THE SOUND OF SILENCE

One moment there had been the thudding roar, which seemed to take her body and vibrate throughout the tunnel and the next, there was silence.

The strangest thing of all was that it seemed *loud*. Her ears began to ache. She went dizzy. She felt herself swaying, and straightened up with an effort. She *listened* but could hear nothing. She held herself very still and was suddenly aware of a faint sound: the whisper of her own breathing. . . .

"An unusual ending . . . one of the wonderful Dr. Palfrey series!"—*New Orleans Times-Picayune*

Also by
JOHN CREASEY

THE UNBEGOTTEN

THE INSULATORS
JOHN CREASEY

MANOR
BOOKS
INC.

Dedication

This book is dedicated to my son Colin, who knows so much more than I can ever do about radio-activity and crystallography.

The idea first came, indeed, when he was showing me over the research laboratory at Cardiff University where he worked.

I doubt if he had any conception of the admiration and the pride I felt that day.

And still do.

A MANOR BOOK 1975

Manor Books Inc.
432 Park Avenue South
New York, New York 10016

Library of Congress Catalog Card Number: 72-95773

Contents

BOOK I

The Project

I

The Noise

"I CAN'T STAND THIS noise," Paul Taylor cried. "It's driving me mad!"

And he both looked and sounded as if he were beside himself, normally pleasant face distorted, mild grey eyes glaring, skin pale to ashen, hands clenched and body quivering. He stood at the window of a small room in a factory laboratory in the north of England, on a mezzanine floor built in one corner overlooking the main machine shop.

A dozen machines were there, embedded in the concrete floor, throbbing, throbbing, throbbing. The floor shook. The walls shook. The ceiling shook. And the roar was constant, never slackening, never ceasing. It was like the growl deep in the throat of an enormous creature; just as it never grew less, so it never grew louder.

Men stood at the machines or moved among them, some actually mouthing words into little mouthpieces built into the machines; one man's face broke into a broad, idiot-grin as he said something while at another machine a man threw back his head and roared with laughter, which did not sound above the roar. Each man wore a kind of ear-muff, to keep out not the cold but the noise.

Rurrr-hurrr — Rurrr-hurr — Rurrr . . .

Up here, on the half-floor, Paul Taylor swung round, clenched hands shaking above his head, face even more distorted; and he mouthed the words again and again. "I can't stand it. I can't stand it. I can't stand it!" The other three men and a girl stopped work at their benches and watched him as he strode towards the door. The girl, dark-haired and with enormous brown eyes which touched a plain, broad-featured face with beauty, put down a set of white porcelain or glass-ceramic insulators and stepped across to Taylor. She wore a knee-length white smock which only hinted at her figure but showed attractive legs and ankles.

Taylor went out and slammed the door; but the noise of the slam was drowned by the roar.

One of the men mouthed words which the girl picked up by inference or lip-reading; she could not possibly hear them.

"Don't follow him, Janey."

Her fingers were on the white glass-ceramic of the handle, and for a moment she hesitated, then, in deliberate defiance, she opened the door and went outside into a long, narrow, grey-painted passage, which was more like a tunnel with its arched ceiling and windowless walls. The noise was less, here; so was the reverberation; but there was still a dull roar like a wall against the ears, and still a-quiver, as if movement was coming from the centre of the earth.

Taylor stood by the far end of the tunnel, leaning against the wall, head bent, face buried in his hands. Slowly, Jane Wylie approached him and put a hand on his shoulder; a hand as beautifully shaped as her legs.

He shook it off, roughly.

She moved in front of him, so that when he looked up he could not fail to see her; and she did not move or touch him again. In her eyes there was such deep compassion. They stood like that for a long time, until suddenly, in a muted explosion, Taylor spat:

"I can't stand it any more!"

Jane didn't speak, but waited in silence until at last he lowered his hands from his face and stared at her, tears streaking his cheeks, his eyes lack-lustre against his flushed face.

"I tell you I can't," he muttered.

"I know how you feel," she tried to soothe.

"No you don't!" he denied petulantly. "Nobody possibly could! If you knew how I felt you wouldn't be able to bear it, either." When she didn't speak or move to touch him he went on in a louder voice, "It seems to start inside me, that's the awful thing. It's as if someone planted a dynamo inside my body and I can't switch it off. *Do you understand that*?" he almost screamed. "It's inside me! It doesn't matter where I am, who I'm with, it's there all the time. I can't leave it behind me *ever*. I tell you it's driving me mad!"

"You need some rest," she still soothed. "Some rest and —"

"I can't sleep, I can't sit back and read, if I watch television I feel as if the set's going to blow up. I've got to get away, I tell you. I can't stay here any longer."

"Paul," Jane Wylie said. "You must."

"But I can't!" he screamed. Now his lips were drawn back over his teeth, very white except where one incisor was gold-capped, and his face still very flushed, as if he had high fever. "I simply can't stay!"

"They won't let you go."

"Then I'll have to run away!"

"They won't let you," she insisted.

"They'll bloody well have to!"

"Paul," said Jane Wylie. "You must ask for a holiday, a week or two away from here will do you a world of good. They might let you go for as short a time as that."

"You know they wouldn't," he sobbed. "You said yourself they'd never let anyone go from this awful place. I'll have to escape." Suddenly he moved forward and gripped her hands so tightly that she winced; but she did not draw back. "Janey! You won't tell them, will you. Promise you won't tell them!"

"I won't tell them a thing," she promised, and then she began not to free her hands but to return his grip very firmly.

The compassion in her eyes seemed to be touched with pain. "But they will find out, you must realise that."

"They can't know if you don't tell them!" He thrust himself forward again, snatched his hands away and thrust them, fingers crooked, towards her throat. "Swear you won't tell them, or I'll choke the life out of you."

His cold fingers touched her warm flesh, and began to press.

Jane Wylie did not move, nor did she try to protect herself; instead, she stood there as if a willing victim. She could feel the vibrations coming from his fingers, he was indeed a man obsessed, a man in deadly fear. The pressure grew tighter, the vibration fiercer, the noise seemed worse than when they had come into this passage, as if a door or a window had opened to let more noise in.

And a door had opened.

At the end of the passage behind Paul Taylor, but in front of Jane, a small man appeared. He was not a dwarf; not even a miniature man; yet his size and stature made him immediately noticeable. He was thin and dressed in a pale grey suit so perfect a fit that it was as if it had been built on to him. He wore a purple turtle-neck sweater beneath the jacket, which was cut in a wide V but had narrow lapels.

Standing motionless, with Taylor's hands tight about her neck, Jane saw him, and started. If Taylor realised something had made her jump he did not show it, but the pressure of his fingers grew tighter, the twist of his lips grew more vicious, the glistening in his eyes was demoniac.

"You won't tell them!" he ground out. "I won't let you, I —"

For the first time, she moved. Very quickly, effortlessly, she did the one thing she could to make sure that he let her go: she brought her knee up into his groin with sharp impact. He gave a choking gasp, let go, staggered back and then bent double. He did not fall but leaned against the wall, drawing in his breath in little squealing sounds.

The man from the end of the passage approached quickly

yet quietly; all his movements were precise. He had regular
features but none was outstanding, he was not handsome.
His complexion was sallow, such as that of a man who spent
most of his time indoors. His eyes were pale grey, and not
so much lifeless as preoccupied.

"Are you all right?" he asked, above Taylor's heavy
breathing.

"Yes," she said. "Perfectly."

"Why did you wait so long before defending yourself?"

"I hoped he would stop without being forced to."

"I see." The man's voice was flat and unemotional; it
seemed strange that he could talk in such a conversational,
matter-of-fact way. "Has he been behaving like this for
long?"

"Don't you know?" Jane asked.

The other did not speak at once. There was no disapproval
in his expression and yet there was a sense of disapproval in
his manner and in his words, which came out very deliberately.

"Whether I know or not is beside the point, Jane. I asked
you a question and I expect an answer. I will repeat the
question: has he been like this for long?"

"He is worse today than I have ever known him," Jane
answered stiffly.

"How long has he been showing signs of emotional
strain?"

"I've noticed it for about a month," she answered; but
in fact it had been for a much longer period, although no-
one could prove *that*.

"Yet you did not report it?" he observed.

She hesitated for what seemed a very long time.

As they had talked and now as she waited, two things
became apparent. The roar of noise was subdued again,
because the door through which the man had come had
closed and latched of its own accord. At the same time the
gasping and wheezing of Taylor's breathing had almost
stopped, and although he still leaned, crouching against the

wall, his body was still. He did not look up, and showed no
sign that he was aware of the fact that they were discussing
him as if he had no idea they were there.

Jane Wylie was ·aware of the tension in him; and she was
afraid, both for him and for herself.

At last, she answered: "I didn't report to you because I
had assumed that you would already be aware of it."

"I see. I also see that you need reminding that your
loyalty should be absolute. If you are aware of any situation
which might affect the efficiency of a colleague and so the
effectiveness of your department, you should report it." He
paused, only to ask very sharply, "Have you discussed this
with any of the others in your department?"

"No," she answered.

"Are they aware of Taylor's emotional sickness?"

"I don't know. I haven't discussed it with them, nor have
they mentioned it to me."

The man said, "Very well." Then he shifted his position
slightly, and looked at Paul Taylor.

Jane was suddenly, vividly conscious of the way Professor
Capelli, the head research chemist, would sometimes look
at rats or rabbits or any creature on which he was experimenting. It was with absolute coldness and indifference: he
saw the animal not as a living creature but as an inanimate
object; and that was how this man was looking at Taylor
now. That was bad enough, but far worse was the fact that
Taylor was obviously aware of it. He began to shiver, and
seemed compelled to look up into the man's face, as if the
other's effect was mesmeric. He did not glance towards Jane,
just stared with pathetic helplessness at the other man. His
eyes were filled with mute appeal, as if he knew it was not
worth putting into words.

Jane felt sudden, awful panic.

It was as if she were watching a man being sentenced to
death.

That was nonsense! Utterly ridiculous. And yet the
thought affected her breathing, which became faster and

more shallow. Suddenly, aware of this physical effect, the sense of panic grew worse, for if her breathing became excited, then she would be seen as emotional, and they had no use for people who allowed their emotions to get out of control.

Gradually, Taylor began to straighten up and for the first time he tried to speak.

"I — " he began, gulped, and tried again. "I — I'm all — " he stopped, seemed to fight for breath, and then actually shouted, "I'm all right!" Now he was upright, fists clenched, eyes staring, and the small man was so intent on him that Jane dared to hope that he had not noticed her agitated breathing.

"I'm all right!" Taylor insisted, this time much more quietly, but there was less doubt than ever of his fear.

"I am very glad to hear it," replied the small man. "Why did you come out of the laboratory?"

"I — I needed some fresh air."

"The air in the laboratory, as in the rest of the plant, is perfectly air-conditioned, as you know quite well."

"That — that's not the same." A streak of defiance showed in Taylor and his voice sharpened. "You know it's not."

"I know you lied to me," the small man accused.

Taylor's eyes blazed.

"I didn't lie!"

"I will ask you the question once again," said the small man in a tone which suggested that his patience was nearly at an end. "Why did you come out of the laboratory?"

Taylor didn't answer at once, but stood in miserable defiance. If he gave a different reason then, he would have been caught in a lie; if he gave the same one then he wouldn't be believed. It was the kind of dilemma in which everyone who worked here, who served those in command, was likely to find himself. Sooner or later everyone seemed to be pushed into such a position with a remorselessness which was the most ruthless thing she had ever known.

Taylor drew in a hissing breath.

"It was the noise," he muttered.

"Speak up, man. I didn't hear you."

Taylor raised both hands, which were clenched as they had been when he had placed them about Jane's throat. He was only a foot or two away from the small man, and trembling violently. It seemed to Jane in those moments of sheer terror that he would attack the man as he had attacked her, and she was quite sure that if he did, he would receive no mercy and might be made to suffer terribly.

He was glaring; his lips were working; his shivering grew worse; he was like that for a long time, then slowly he began to slacken and relax until his arms fell by his side and the tightness at his lips eased.

He muttered, "It was the noise."

"Louder," ordered the small man.

A few notes higher but now without showing any kind of resentment, Taylor repeated what he had said in a tone of great clarity.

"What don't you like about the noise?" the other demanded.

"It gives me a headache."

"Have you ever reported this?"

"No," Taylor answered, his voice falling again. "No."

"Why not?"

"I — I thought — I thought you would disapprove."

"You *thought*! Why didn't you find out? What made you think that we are inhuman creatures, indifferent to your well-being?" When Taylor did not answer the man barked, "Is that what you thought?"

"I — I — no!" He was beginning to gasp again. "No, it isn't!"

"Then why didn't you come to me for help?"

Now, Paul was standing again in that aggressive stance, hands clenched and held in front of his chest, chin out, shoulders thrusting forward. For the second time Jane felt the rise of panic like a suffocating pressure within her. If Paul struck him, the little man would become a devil.

"Now don't be silly," the little man said, sharply, but in a not unfriendly way. "You need a rest, and you shall have one. No one can work for ever without a break." For him, he was quite jovial. "Now, come along, Taylor — fetch your personal things from the laboratory, and come with me."

Paul did not hesitate; it was as if the little man had subdued all resistance, all fight, and so all spirit and courage. When they went into the laboratory the other three glanced up but made no comment. Paul simply collected a few oddments — pens, a pen-knife, some keys and loose change, took off his smock, and walked out in the little man's wake.

He did not say goodbye; he did not look at the others, not even at Jane. Perhaps the worst thing of all was that when the door had closed, no-one made a single word of comment. Yet Jane felt like screaming, out of a dreadful fear that she would never see Paul Taylor again.

2

Woman Alone

JANE WYLIE WENT to her section of the long bench set against a window which stretched along one side of the room. The glass let in the daylight but was itself obscured so that she could not see out, could not be distracted when at work. Beyond, she knew, were peaceful green fields and colourful flowerbeds and, on rising land, a thick wood of oak and beech and birch, fresh with the new green of spring. Had she been able to look out, it would have brought balm; but the frosted-glass window did nothing to ease the fear, the anger and the resentment she felt.

In front of her were dozens of small glass-ceramic tubes in varying sizes, some openings half-an-inch across, some barely an eighth. In each were packed crystals from the super-heated ovens which filled one, narrow end of the room. Every kind of base ore, every kind of metal, every variety of glass was used to make the crystals, which came out of the ovens feather-light. Over in a glass case opposite the bench and at right-angles with the ovens, were specimens of the crystals which had been made during the experiments. She, Janey, could remember the fierce surge of excitement when one crucible had seemed to be full not of ordinary crystals, or quartz, or coloured crystalline pieces, but of diamonds.

"We are not looking for diamonds," Arthur Leadbetter — the Chief Chemist — had told her coldly.

He moved towards her as she picked up one of the tubes, and the shadow of his tall figure fell upon her bench. Her heart began to thump, she knew she must look up and see him but could not make herself, until he said:

"Janey."

She looked round, and up at him. He was six foot three or four, with a very lean body and a long thin face with a pointed chin. He gave the impression of having been squeezed before he set into his present shape. His eyes were heavy-lidded and had dark patches, as if he were desperately in need of sleep.

"Yes, Arthur," she responded at last.

"I shall need those batches in an hour's time."

"I'll be ready," she promised.

"Make sure you are," he said severely.

Had the small man spoken like that, he would have sounded sinister. Leadbetter didn't; instead, he sounded rather sad. He was trying to speak to her with his eyes, too, as if pleading. She knew what he meant; he was begging her not to lose her temper, not to show sympathy for Paul. He was frightened, too; he always had been. He wanted 'them' to believe he was being severe, for this whole place was bugged; but his severity was unconvincing and even pathetic, being born out of fear.

All of them were frightened.

Freddie Ferris, over at the glass-doored ovens, looking in, was checking the temperature. Those ovens could be taken up to 4,000° Fahrenheit; far beyond fusion point for the hardest of metals. Freddie was sandy-skinned and red-haired, freckled and chubby; even after being here so long he retained his pink colour and his fat, and his white smock was a shade too tight for him. When he had first come here he had been full of fun, the life and soul of the party, as it were, but never wearisome.

It must be a week since Janey had seen him smile.

Philip Carr, at the radiation unit at the other end of the

laboratory, was normally a solemn and earnest individual, and Jane was not sure whether he had changed inwardly or not. Outwardly he was the same: precise, rather over-formal, speaking in a pleasing 'Oxford' accent, very courteous and conscientious. He was remarkably adept in manoeuvring the mechanical arms which clawed the radio-active material inside the lead and porcelain 'ovens'. He had developed the use of these until it was almost as if he were using his own fingers, placing pieces of crystal-filled glass-ceramic in a dozen different places. Carr was a man of medium height and medium build. His dark hair, always cut short, always seemed exactly the same; the hair showed up his tan, and he looked as if he had just come from the ski-slopes or the sun lamp. Even in his smock he appeared immaculate; certainly he was the best groomed of all the research chemists here.

Janey went on with her work, which was simple yet very exacting. She had to pack crystals from each batch manu-factured in the ovens into the glass ceramic tubes, with a piece of lead foil between each two batches; and she had to tag the lead foil with an identification number. The tubes would then be lowered one after another into one of the testing chambers, and submitted to a full charge of radio-activity which would melt the lead if the crystals did not insulate the paper-thin foil.

Some crystals did give a kind of protection; a built-in timing device told how long it was before the lead-foil actually melted. One set of crystals had resisted the radio-activity for over an hour, but eventually the foil had melted. The crystals were cheap to manufacture and very light; once a batch could be used as insulators against radio-activity then significant progress would have been made in protecting people and instruments from the effects of radio-active contamination.

There had been a great deal of experimental work in crystallography in this search for an insulator in industrial as well as State-controlled research, not only in Great

Britain but throughout the world. There was no way of being sure which country or which industrial unit was nearest a breakthrough. The certain thing was that once a breakthrough was made, then the industrial as well as the military use of nuclear energy would be vastly cheaper and easier. If the first breakthrough was made by a commercial company or group then it would be able to quote ridiculously low prices for nuclear reactors and nuclear powering of all kinds of machines, from aeroplanes to submarines and trains to merchant ships.

Janey, at the time intensely interested in the practical aspects of crystallography, had answered an advertisement for a research physicist with some knowledge of the subject. She had been told at the third interview, before being offered the job, that it would be done under conditions of the most stringent secrecy; that she herself would have to be screened with infinite care to make sure that she was not a spy for some other group engaged in the same research.

"You will have to devote yourself exclusively to The Project," she had been told by a man not unlike the small one in charge here, but bigger and more aggressive in his manner. "You will have to live in the restricted area of The Project, and will have no physical contact with the outside world during the year you are on The Project. But there are excellent facilities at the Company's headquarters . . ."

She had been shown a short film in colour, of the grounds in which the research buildings were set, and it was explained that a model industrial city had been planned here, and partly constructed, before a change of government had diverted the funds, and a group of research organisations, it was said, had taken over.

They saw pictures of the sweeping lawns sloping down to a small river, where there were boats and jetties and places on the banks for fishing; there was a lido for swimming and sun-bathing and deck or beach games, a big indoor swimming-pool and gymnasium. There was a small cinema, a theatre with seats for five hundred people, an auditorium for orchestras. Everything for pleasure as well as cultural facilities was there; a library, bookshop, record shop — a small shopping centre for those who preferred to cook for themselves. Many of the married couples preferred this.

"What you do in your personal life is no concern of ours," Parsons had said, and with almost startling frankness he had added, "If you wish to sleep with one of your fellow workers, whether you prefer promiscuity to a settled sexual relationship will be entirely a matter for you to decide."

He had meant that: in fact events had proved that he had meant everything he had said.

There were faithful married couples and also there were community groups which changed partners whenever the mood took them. There were groups of male homosexuals and, as she had discovered with surprisingly little sense of revulsion, there were lesbians in one of the little apartment communities. It was as if those who controlled The Project knew that the unnatural segregation from the outside world meant that some degree of perversion was inevitable, and knew also that if a man or a woman's sexual proclivities were released the discipline necessary for the work could be more easily imposed.

Most of the workers, once they had served for a year signed on for another. Others simply disappeared, presumably going back to the outside world.

She had now been here for six months, half of her contract period. There were times when she was quite content but other times when she felt that she was being suffocated, that this was a prison and she would never sign on for another year.

Paul Taylor had begun contentedly enough, until the noise had become too much for him. One either got used to the noise or eventually succumbed to it. She got used to the constant roaring, and no longer used the ear-plugs which were standard equipment.

She was not sure why so much noise was necessary. No real attempt was made to muffle it; there were times when she felt that it was deliberately imposed, so as to deaden feeling.

She thought all these things as she prepared the crystal containers and placed them in neat piles by her right hand. There were only a few left to do, and she would be finished in good time.

Freddie Ferris came across and shot her a quick sideways glance as he said,

"Have you enough crystals?"

"Plenty, Freddie," she answered.

"I can easily bring you more."

"No, I've plenty," she insisted.

He moved a little closer to her and took a handful of the crystals from a transparent bowl on her left. He peered at these as if he were examining them, and spoke out of the side of his mouth.

"*Do you think Paul will ever come back?*" The whisper was barely audible above the roar from the generating room.

"Of course he will!" she answered sharply.

"*Don't raise your voice!*" Freddie urged, and when she glanced at him from the corner of her eyes, he went on: "I don't think he will." He looked expressionless except for what might be dread in his eyes.

She did not think Paul would come back but she said quickly: "Nonsense!"

"*I don't think we'll ever get out of here alive,*" Freddie mouthed. "No-one does and no-one ever will."

"Nonsense," she repeated. "Of course we shall."

"*I don't believe it. I believe they'll keep us here as long as we're useful to them, and then kill us.*"

She felt a rising, choking dread, yet replied with a calm which surprised her. "What on earth makes you feel that?"

"*I just feel it,*" he said. "*I'm terrified out of my wits.*"

"I think the noise is getting on your nerves," she retorted. "Try to forget it, Freddie."

"*Forget it!*" he exclaimed, and let the crystals fall back into the bowl. As they fell he looked up at her with impassioned appeal, his very heart seemed to show in his eyes: "*Janey! Don't tell anyone I said this.*"

"Of course I won't, you oaf," Janey assured him.

Then she was aware of Leadbetter approaching, betrayed by a pale shadow on the translucent glass of the window. She placed the last of her batch of little containers on the bench, and then turned away from Freddie and looked up into Leadbetter's face. There was nothing to suggest disapproval, or that the Chief Chemist had heard what they had been discussing.

"Are you ready?" he asked.

"Yes — all done," she answered. "One hundred and twenty."

"Good. Philip is ready," Leadbetter told her. "Freddie and I will take them over. You go and rest, Janey. You look tired."

She wasn't tired; she was very frightened, and tense with trying to hide it, and her fear grew worse when she realised that he had noticed something was wrong. She did not want to be questioned or scrutinised, so she turned quickly away as Philip came up with some containers for the little tubes. He looked at her without expression; it was easy to believe that he was disapproving.

She went out by the door through which Paul Taylor had gone. There were doors at either end of the tunnel-like passage, and also some in the wall, like this one. Opposite was another, leading to a passage with a common-room for relaxation, with a bar and coffee stand, so one could have whatever one felt like. The big, pleasant room usually had half-a-dozen people in it, sometimes from the other departments and from the laboratory, and there was usually a lot of gossip — about one another and the staff, but never about The Project.

This afternoon, the room was empty, thank God!

She went across to the coffee stand, where there was always fresh coffee and found herself a cup, added cream but no sugar, and went across to the window and looked out on lawns and the river, a few people walking, a few even sitting and talking. The sun was bright in a pale but cloudless sky. This was why the room was deserted; it was warm enough, for once, to go outside.

If she went out she would have to talk, which was the last thing she wanted to do. She pulled up a comfortable chair and sat, drank coffee and tried to calm her nerves. The awful thing was her fear that Freddie was right, that Paul Taylor would be killed. And yet how could such a fear be justified? The place was getting on her nerves.

But there was the other underlying fear: that they *would* all be killed whenever their period of usefulness was over; that this was the last era of their lives — of *her* life. Nothing actually gave her cause to believe this, but it was a feeling which came like a lightning flash, and it was never possible to reject it absolutely. Now she knew that Freddie shared the fear; as if the idea was not in her mind but in the very atmosphere of the place.

If Paul came back to the laboratory, they would all be reassured, they could laugh at themselves! But if he didn't, then her fears and Freddie's would be taken to a pitch of almost intolerable tension.

She found herself wondering whether Leadbetter had overheard Freddie; whether he was already under suspicion and being closely watched; and then she told herself what was obviously true; they were *all* watched, *all* the time.

She had another cup of coffee, freshened up in the powderroom, then went back to the tunnel-passage. As she stepped into it and closed the door, something happened, something utterly unbelievable, something which had never happened here before.

Silence fell.

One moment there had been the thudding roar which

seemed to take her body, and vibrate throughout the tunnel
as well as the common-room and the laboratory, the next
there was silence.

The strangest thing of all was that it seemed *loud.*

Nearly as strange, the vibration was still as great as ever.
Her ears began to ache. She went dizzy. She felt herself
swaying, and straightened up with an effort. She *listened*
but could hear nothing. She held herself very still and was
suddenly aware of a faint sound: of her own breathing.

She made herself move forward.

Something had happened to destroy her equilibrium. She
staggered, and stretched out her hand to the wall, for support.
Leaning against the wall, she edged towards the laboratory
door. It was closed; of course it was closed! She reached it
and, with great care, took the handle in her fingers, turned
and pushed. The door opened and she stepped inside.

The three men were all near the radio-active units,
Leadbetter in the middle, the other two on either side,
Philip's body swivelled round so that he could stare at his
chief, and Freddie's lips actually parted, as if he had been
struck dumb in the middle of a sentence.

No-one spoke.

There was no sound except the one which came slowly
into Janey's consciousness: the whisper of their own breathing.
Slowly, the men looked at one another and then turned to
look at Janey, utterly amazed at what had fallen upon them.

And the vibration went on and on.

Leadbetter's lips moved and he made a faint croaking
sound. Freddie mouthed two simple words: "*Oh, God.*"
Philip raised a hand in front of his face and snapped thumb
and forefinger and the snap seemed very loud.

Then as suddenly as the noise had stopped it began again;
this time it was like thunder, roaring and reverberating in
their ears.

Something had cut out the sound; had insulated the

building *against* the sound. That was the most astounding thing of all. For the machines had gone on working or there would have been no vibration.

By some miracle, the sound had been eliminated; had gone completely.

3

The Fears

ALL FOUR OF the group stood still as statues for perhaps two minutes, and then began to relax very slowly. It was Philip Carr who spoke first, with much more animation than usual.

"What the devil was that?"

"It was uncanny," gasped Ferris.

"As if the noise was switched off," put in Janey.

"It couldn't have been switched — " began Philip, only to stop as Freddie burst out:

"You mean the machines couldn't have been switched off and then on again so swiftly; there would have been a phasing of the noise?"

"Could it have been a deliberate experiment?" asked Janey, fighting down her excitement. "Aren't we looking for new forms of insulation? Why not of noise?"

"It could have been a breakdown," Freddie almost screeched. "The Project generates its own electricity, it doesn't feed from the grid or the Electricity Board's supply."

"There's never been anything like it, we do know that," Philip declared, looking at Leadbetter. "What do *you* think, Charles?"

Leadbetter was standing back from them all, cheeks pale, the patches under his eyes very black, the heavy lids half covering the eyes themselves. He looked shocked, and moistened his lips several times before he spoke. His Adam's apple jerked up and down.

"It must have been an electrical failure," he stated.

"But if the ovens lose heat —" began Freddie.

"And the vibrations —" Philip started.

"Never mind the guessing!" cried Leadbetter, and two spots of colour appeared like burns on his cheeks. "We've our work to do, and we don't want to fall behind. Get to it, both of you. Janey! You tidy up Freddie's desk, please, as well as Paul's. Take everything out of Paul's and put it in a container."

Fear stabbed afresh at Janey, overshadowing the excitement she had felt at first. If noise *had* been insulated it was a major scientific and industrial breakthrough and should be a cause of great rejoicing. Instead, Leadbetter was frightened, and what he had said obviously shocked the other men.

Philip, already on the move to his section of the desk, spun round. Freddie's hands clenched and raised in front of his chest.

"Why tidy up *Paul's* desk?" Philip demanded.

Leadbetter said sharply: "He won't be coming back."

"My *God*!" breathed Freddie, looking at Janey, horror struck. "Why not?"

"Don't ask questions," Leadbetter replied shrilly. "Get on with your job."

He raised a clenched hand threatening, as if he would actually strike the others. The two burning spots seemed to grow bigger and fiercer. Janey felt her heart beating fast enough to suffocate her, yet she didn't turn away. Freddie seemed to fade into the background as conflict struck between the other two men.

"Charles," Philip said coldly, "we are not slaves."

"You're paid to work, not gossip. And paid extremely well."

"I do my work as well as any man, and you know it." Philip drew a deep breath, and there was open defiance in his manner. "I want to know why Paul isn't coming back."

"He is being retired," Leadbetter answered roughly.

"What does 'retired' mean?"

"That has nothing to do with you."

"It has everything to do with me," Philip asserted icily. "The day might come when I am retired, and I want to know what would happen to me. So I want to know what has happened to Paul."

"He's not well. I tell you he's been retired. For God's sake get on with the job!" All the colour had faded from Leadbetter's face and his eyes showed feverishly bright. Philip, on the other hand, looked normal and calmly determined. Janey, looking on helplessly, realised that this was the second conflict with authority in the laboratory in a few hours. The small man had been aware of the first from the beginning. Was he also aware of this?

The small man, whose name was Ashley, sat at a desk in a large, circular room in the centre of the complex of buildings, a room in a tower rather like that of an airport control. Several television sets were built into the wall opposite his desk, and he was watching one intently. So was the man Parsons, who had hired Janey and the others. There was no sound in the room except the voices of the people in the laboratory, and these came through with great clarity. The picture on the screen was perfect, every line, every blemish on the faces of the people there showed up. So did the fear and the anxiety.

Philip Carr was saying, "What does 'retired' mean?"

And Leadbetter cried, "That has nothing to do with you!"

"It's everything to do with me," retorted Philip icily.

For a few moments it looked as if the conflict would become physical, as if the two men would start fighting. But suddenly and unexpectedly Philip Carr gave way, turned abruptly and went to the nuclear ovens, and began to move those pincer-like claws. The glass-ceramic containers were fed into the nuclear chamber by a series of automatic movements which was absolutely safe. Then, Philip began to manipulate the test articles with unbelievable dexterity. The thers turned and moved back to their desks, as if resignedly. The hidden television camera showed only their profiles and the backs of their heads and shoulders. The sounds coming out now were faint clicks of metal on metal or ceramic on ceramic.

Ashley said, "Taylor's defection has affected them all."

Parsons, simply a larger edition of the other man, said, "It certainly looks like that."

"What shall we do?"

"We shall have to report it," answered Parsons.

"We can make a recommendation," remarked Ashley drily.

"What would your recommendation be?" asked Parsons.

"I would point out that Philip Carr is brilliant at his job, quite the best man we have."

"Ah. And Leadbetter?"

"I do not think he would yield under pressure, either."

"The woman?"

"I think she is competent, and that her nerve will not break."

Parsons nodded, very slowly. The soft sounds came from the set, and the roaring, rumbling sound filled this office just as it filled every passage and every corner of The Project. All of the scientists in the laboratory were working now, and suddenly the automatic camera revealed that the way Philip handled the manipulator arms of the ovens was quite remarkable.

At last, Ashley said, "But there is Ferris."

"What do you think of him?"

"That he is thoroughly unreliable and must be removed."

"But the members of the group have such feeling for one another."

"They live in constant if subdued anxiety for themselves, and when it comes to a choice they will always prefer to save their own lives than to make sacrifices for others," Ashley replied. "I think Ferris must go, and I don't think the others will be distressed. And we must put other men in his place and in Taylor's. When the changes have been made we can

see how the new mixture works as a team. We can in any
case find out whether the disrupting force is one or both of
the men who have gone, or one of those who has been left
behind."

"Whom would you suspect?" asked Parsons sharply.

"Taylor and Ferris," Ashley said promptly. "I think we
should remove Ferris at once; the others will then have only
the one shock to withstand, which will be much better than
two with a gap in between." He paused before asking, "Shall
I report? Or will you?

"You report." Ashley answered; he made it seem much
less a concession than a command, there was no doubt which
man was in control. "We don't want to lose Carr or Wylie
since they are both exceptionally good at their specific jobs."

Parsons nodded, but seemed to have some doubt; and after
a few moments Ashley asked sharply:

"Why are you objecting?"

"I'm wondering if there is a way to persuade them all to
do what they're told without asking questions," said Parsons,
musingly. "At the moment they are both obviously tense
and edgy, and could be easily frightened. Which is better:
to go on as if we have noticed nothing, and hope that the
fact that they don't run into trouble eases their fears: or to
give them a sharp lesson, disciplining them by fear?"

Ashley's face looked almost razor sharp as he considered
the other man, and it was some time before he asked:

"What have you in mind as a sharp lesson?"

"Letting them know that Taylor is dead."

"How?"

"By allowing them to come upon his body, or —"

"Oh, nonsense!"

"Very well, then," said Parsons, quite amiably. "By
taking a photograph of the body and enabling them to see it
as if by chance. This particular laboratory is the most important we have: workers have been allowed to leave other
departments but here, where the insulation by crystals is in
such an advanced stage of research, we can take no risks.

If it comes to a point they will have to be forced to work as we wish them to. Is this the time to begin the forcing?"

Ashley's subsequent pause lasted much longer, and when he moved and spoke, it was with some approval.

"I will make the suggestion to Birch," he stated. "And of course I will tell them whence it originated."

"Why, thank you," said Parsons, and his voice sounded smooth yet his tone laconic. "I'll be very interested to know what they say."

Janey had a restless evening and as restless a night.

She went to a film, a Swedish one with sub-titles in English, although the contortions of the passionate hero and heroine needed no language; there never was a clearer case of actions speaking louder than words. Coming out, she saw Philip approaching from the common-room and wondered if he had been waiting for her. Here, in the open, there was less chance of being overheard. Yet Philip asked if she had enjoyed the film, tried to behave as if there were nothing on his mind, until they were out of earshot of anyone else in the grounds. Then he said abruptly,

"I think we were watched tonight."

"I sensed it, too," Janey said.

"Janey — how is your nerve?"

"Bad," she replied. "I feel — somehow I feel like a prisoner here, as if something's going on that I don't understand. Do you know what I mean?"

"Yes," he answered. "And it's a great pity your nerve is so bad."

"Why?" she demanded.

"I thought you might be prepared to take the risk of escaping," Philip told her. "I like it here at The Project less and less." When Janey didn't answer immediately he asked softly, "Well? Do you feel like finding out what would happen if we just walked out?"

"No," she answered, almost piteously. "No."

He did not try to persuade her, just shrugged and gripped

her arm for a moment; and then, to her surprise, slipped his arm round her waist. Philip had always been aloof; she had sometimes wondered whether sex interested him at all. She felt his hand firm and yet gentle on her breast as he guided her away from the main building towards the river. A few other couples were about, as well as three or four small parties. It was the mildest night of the year so far and bright, too, with a waning moon on its back with a faint haze of cloud passing beneath it. She didn't speak; did not attempt to move his hand. When they were close to the river bank at a spot where the moon as well as stars were reflected in the gurgling water he went on,

"Will you help me to?"

"What?"

"Don't be dense, Janey. Will you help me to escape?" After a moment there was a note of mockery in his voice. "Or are you too afraid for that, too?"

"Are you really sure it *is* a prison?" she demanded, and he paused for a while before answering:

"I've come to the conclusion that it isn't what we thought when we came — a kind of consortium of big industrialists who want the work done secretly. I feel as if every move I make is watched, every word I say overheard — except out here in the open. I want to go and see the situation from the outside. Have you nerve enough to help?"

"Yes," she said quietly. "If there is a safe way for you, I'll help. Philip —"

"Don't make conditions," he pleaded.

"Philip, when did you first think of leaving?"

"It's been in and out of my mind for weeks," he told her.

"Good gracious! I would have thought you were the last one to be thinking of it. You seemed so — satisfied."

"The better to fool Big Brother with," he said lightly. "I have now placed myself well and truly into your hands, sweet lass. One murmur from you to Ashley or Parsons, and all hope for me will be gone."

"You know I won't talk," she said, half-resentfully, looking at his profile. She was acutely aware of the gentle pressure of his hand. "How can I help?"

"You really will?"

"Of course I will. I — I've been worried for some time, too."

"Then this is how you can help," he said, and he drew her closer until their bodies touched and his arm was very firm about her. "You can pretend to have succumbed to my charms. You can come and spend the night with me or I can come and spend it with you. We shall talk of nothing except passion and love-making, we shall ooh and ah, and giggle and quip, like any pair of lovers. We might be more convincing if we let all our inhibitions go and did the real thing, without pretending, but that I leave to you. If I come to you or *vice versa* for a few nights, then they are likely to see us as cooing doves likely to become permanent mates." She had never known him talk so freely, and with this light and amusing tone. "Once we are known as lovers, they will never be sure which bed we shall be in, and as they told us with such endearing frankness when we enlisted, they will care less. Whenever I am not in my bed they will assume I am in yours." He squeezed, gently, and went on, "Delectable thought. Delectable prospect, if only you will share it."

"And when you have deflowered me you will fly away," said Janey, drily.

"Oh, my dear," he said, startled. And then almost in alarm he went on, "Janey, if it really would be a complete beginning, I — I — Good God! Forget the whole thing." He took his hand away quickly and they walked side by side in the moonlight; for the first time, her heart began to beat very fast. At last he gave a hollow kind of laugh and went on in a tone of great dismay: "I will gladly sleep in a chair in your kitchen, or — " his voice rose as if with inspiration: "In the bath! Now why didn't I think of that before?"

"Philip," Janey said, "why didn't you let me know you could be such an idiot?"

"You must blame my natural shyness," Philip retorted; and then he whispered so that she could only just hear the words. "We're being followed. Don't mind what I do." On the instant he took her in his arms and their bodies were locked, and it was as if fire ran through her. He held her in such a way that her thighs were close to his, her bosom too, but her head was back, pale in that lovely light; and he bent forward and placed his open lips against hers in a kiss which seemed to draw the very breath out of her body.

She was not aware of it, but two men passed as they embraced; and soon afterwards, two women.

"So he went to her apartment," Ashley said with satisfaction. "Good."

"Why so good?" asked Parsons.

"Oh, don't be absurd," rasped Ashley. "If they are having a passionate love affair, they will be much more inclined to get through their work quickly, living for the evenings or for the weekends. I don't think we need let them see Taylor's body, after all."

4

Lovers

JANEY FELT A quickening sense of excitement as they walked from the grounds towards her apartment block. Hers consisted of two rooms with a little kitchen recess, maintained by the organisation's staff; whenever she cooked herself a meal here instead of going to the restaurant for the senior employees, the Jamaican maid did the washing-up next morning. In some ways it was a luxurious or at least self-indulgent life. Now and again she threw a cocktail party up here, with everyone from the laboratory as well as a few friends, or rather acquaintances. These might be from the offices, people she had met at the restaurant or at the weekly Project Party, open to everyone of a certain rank. It reminded her of the big Captain's Party on board an ocean liner: everyone from the laboratories was welcome and most made friends.

But this was the first time she had brought a man up with her.

She had never felt anything but tentative liking for Philip, he had always been formal, so intent on his work, so aloof. He had been here when she had come and his first year must nearly be up. She wondered what made him so anxious to escape when he had only a few months to go. She had occasionally wondered whether he looked on her as a woman or simply as a physicist, a creature with two arms and two legs mostly covered by a shapeless white smock, and a head sticking out from the top. Now, his hand was at her waist, prompting rather than pushing.

She opened the door, and dropped her keys, she was so nervous. He picked them up, held the door open, and gave a faintly mocking bow. She went into the big living-room which had a wide window fronting lawns and flowerbeds. She stood looking out, yet was acutely aware of his approach although after the click of the closing door he made hardly any sound. She knew the moment when he was behind her. She felt his arms pass between her body and her arms, and the gentle cupping of her breasts. She began to tremble. Again, he held her in such a position that she could lean her head back against his shoulder, and he held her gently and ran his lips over her cheeks, her lips, her eyes, her forehead. Then he drew back so that she was acutely aware of him.

He let her go.

"Janey," he said. "You are a most exciting woman."

"Philip," she retorted, "the only woman on an island is always exciting."

"I don't agree with you," replied Philip. "In the first place there are plenty of women on this island, some of them — as if you didn't know — here just for the titillation and pleasure of men."

She turned her head; he was very close.

"I really didn't know."

"Then you've kept your eyes closed!"

"Perhaps," she said. "In a way I always have."

"And you want to keep them closed? To be aware of no-one but yourself and your fellow workers. That's how you've always seemed to me."

"Aloof, you mean?" She was astonished.

"Yes."

"Good gracious! It was you who was aloof!"

He laughed and moved so that he could sit on the window ledge and look at her. There was a light from the moon and from the lamps outside, enough to see her clearly, although his face was in shadow. But his head and shoulders and lean body were sharp and dark against the window. He hugged one knee.

"I regarded you as untouchable," he told her. "Unapproachable, too. And I always knew you would be exciting if the barriers could be broken down."

"Thank you, sir," she managed to retort.

"I've never meant anything more — and I've never been more sure," he said.

She simply stood there, her heart racing and her body a-quiver, aware not only of him but of desire. She had not known what toll the months had taken of her, how much he had been in her mind; indeed, how often she had told herself it was absurd to think of him, he was so aloof.

"Janey," he said, softly.

"Yes."

"You are not really a virgin, are you?"

She said: "No. Until a year ago, I was married." After a momentary hesitation, she went on, "I was married for five years, in all."

"Ah," he said, and asked softly, "Happily?"

"Very."

"What happened?"

"He — he wasn't so happy as I was."

"Divorce?"

"Yes."

"Oh, Janey," he said, in a tone of dismay. "I'm so sorry. It must have hurt damnably."

"It did hurt, very much. I was so lonely and — and so shattered. I hadn't realised he had fallen out of love, and he didn't want to hurt me."

"The purgatory of married fools," he remarked gently. "So you were lonely and this job attracted you."

"Very much."

"Do you still like this job, as a job?"

. She hesitated, yet knew that she must not, for long. When they had been in the grounds he had told her, in whispers,

that all the apartments and all the departments, the public
rooms, the theatre and the cinema and the clubs, were bugged,
nothing could be said without it being fed into a control
room so that it could be replayed and studied and examined
word by word, not only for the surface meaning but for
nuance, too. Whatever they said in the apartment could be
heard and taped, and they could not talk confidentially, except of themselves. His last words had been, "They won't
mind lovers clucking.'

Now she sensed a stiffening of his body, as if the long
delay worried him, and she herself knew that she had hesitated too long, as if she was not certain whether she liked
The Project. But at last she said:

"In many ways."

"Ah! Not every way?"

"No," she said. "It's very lonely."

"With so many handsome men about? Nonsense!"

"It is lonely," she insisted. "Oh, the working conditions
are wonderful except for the noise and that doesn't worry
me like it does Paul. And the food's very good and one can't
complain of The Project being a cultural desert! But — well,
it's still lonely."

"Does it have to be?" he asked.

"I don't quite understand you," she said, but in fact she
understood very well, and her heart began to gallop again.

"I mean, will you be so lonely if you and I — " he hesitated, slid off the window ledge, took her hands and drew
her close as he went on, "If you and I became lovers."

He wanted to make love to her, to become lovers, so that
he could escape. That was the one thing she could not say
because it would be overheard, and it was the one thing
which made her hesitate. She was young and free and lonely,
and there was something about him which stirred her as she
had not been stirred for a long time. But he would simply
be using her; as Bruce had used her even though he had been
sleeping with the other woman, planning to leave her when

ever it most suited him although he had sworn it was because he had been so worried about causing her hurt.

Bruce had used her, then, and cast her aside.

This man wanted to use her, and cast her aside.

The difference was that he did not deceive her. She
realised with a sense of shock that he had not said that he
loved her, had not pretended in any way. They would be
lovers until such time as he thought he could escape, and
then she would be alone again. Would the loneliness be better
or worse?

"Janey," he said. "I've tried to take you by storm, and
I know I shouldn't have. You won't hold it against me, will
you?"

"Of course not," she replied, and added with a laugh:
"You did take my breath away!"

"But you soon got it back! Would you like me to go?"

"Oh, please, not yet. Will you have some coffee?"

"I would even have a drink!"

"Oh, dear!" she exclaimed, with a helpless little shrug.
"I don't have any."

"You don't *drink*?"

"Not on my own."

"Good God! And truly, what a woman! Then coffee, by
all means coffee!" He followed her as she put on one or two
table lights, making it brighter but not too bright, and went
through the hall to the kitchen recess. She switched on a per-
colator and then took biscuits from tins — shortbreads from
one, chocolate biscuits from another, plain from the third. The
coffee-pot began to burble and burp, Philip continued to
look at her while leaning against the back of a chair. She was
discovering that he had a habit of leaning back and hugging
his right knee. In this brighter light from a strip of 'daylight'
fluorescence, and at this angle, he was much better looking
than she had realised. He had done something to his hair,
ruffled it a little, and it softened his well-cut, rather severe
features. His well-shaped lips were much more expressive
than she had ever noticed at the office. The expression at

both eyes and lips implied a sense of merriment, as if the situation amused him; and perhaps her attitude did, too.

She had never really fitted the permissive, bed-hopping society, and to a man of the world she might seem far too shy; or coy; or timid. He did not come close to her again and she wished he would, how contrary could one be? When the coffee was ready she carried the tray and he brought a plate of biscuits, and placed them next to the tray. They talked lightly and pleasantly enough but something of the sparkle had gone; perhaps because he had taken 'no' so quickly. He seemed to relish the shortbreads more than the other kinds, and she went to get some more.

When she came back, he wasn't there.

Her heart gave a wild lurch, and she opened her lips to cry out — and on the instant he was behind her but this time his hand was on her lips, pressing firmly, hurting a little. And his lips were close to her ear, whispering.

"Don't make a sound until I tell you." He drew his hand away, but stood very close to her, then he took her wrist and led her to one side of the room and into the bedroom. There he made a loud kissing sound, and, leaving her, sat on the bed and slowly climbed over to the other side.

"Wonderful," he said. And a moment later, "Oh, darling, why did we wait so long." Then he was on the other side of the bed and tip-toeing to the window, beckoning her. Bewildered, even angry, she nevertheless went to him, and he took her hand and pointed towards the far end of the lawns.

There was a man, creeping from one set of bushes to another. Now and again he turned round and looked behind him, obviously in fear of being followed. Suddenly, he straightened up and ran towards this block of flats, and his face showed clearly in the lamplight.

It was Paul Taylor; and he looked terrified.

He was crouching as he ran, as if afraid of being seen, and was looking towards this window as if in despairing hope of succour. He was only forty or fifty yards away, his mouth wide open, the light making his eyes seem dark and bright. At thirty yards he straightened up as if emboldened, and slowed down to a walk.

As he did so, men appeared at the sides.

He saw them, and reared up; and then he spun round and began to run at full pelt back whence he had come. But other men appeared from there and from the sides and quite suddenly he was surrounded. He began to shout and fight, and then all the men began to strike him, with short, stubby sticks held in their right hands. Slowly, he sank down in the midst of them but the men still struck and struck, until he disappeared.

Janey felt Philip's arm about her.

She was cold with horror at what she had seen; and quivering. His arm comforted her. She began to form the words: "It's horrible," but his hand closed over her lips again and he whispered: "Don't make a sound." She continued to shiver. She did not want to watch but there was a mesmeric fascination about the group of men who drew back now; six, in all. Two moved forward as if at a word of command, and picked up Paul's inert body and carried it away.

Janey began to sob.

Philip did not whisper again but, arm firmly about her waist, led her towards the bed, soon now he bade her: "Lie down." She felt him pulling off her shoes, and loosening the high neck of her dress, where it had suddenly become very tight. She felt his hands at her waist, but they did not linger. He eased her on to the bed and then, quite skilfully, pulled blankets and an eiderdown from under her and then rolled them over her, making her into a cocoon. Next he put a hand to her hair and drew the strands away from the gap between neck and pillow, to make her more comfortable. Finally, he hitched himself into a sitting position, and rested one hand on the soft eiderdown. All this time she had shivered with the emotional tension, but gradually she slackened, as she grew

warmer. He put on a bedside light which was not too bright,
and smiled down at her.

"Like some coffee or tea?"

"N-no, thank you."

"Are you warm enough?"

"I will be s-s-soon."

"Good," he said, and there was a funny kind of tone in
his voice when he went on, "It's *very* romantic."

"Oh, Philip," she said. "Please don't joke. That was —
horrible."

"I'm sorry," he said. "I won't pretend it wasn't. I think
it's made one thing clear, though. Only very highly paid
mercenaries would behave with that kind of brutality — or
political fanatics. My bet is that they are political fanatics
but we need not worry about that now." He hitched himself
into a more comfortable position, hand still resting lightly at
her waist. It made a warm spot, there. Her shivering stopped
and for a while they were silent, until suddenly Janey moved,
and took his hand, and drew it inside the covering, warm
upon her breast. She was still horrified and frightened, and
her only comfort was from Philip; and she could see him
looking down at her, smiling faintly. She wanted to shut out
the horror she had seen; she wanted so much to be comforted.

She said in a whisper, "Lie close to me."

He put his lips to her ear and said very, very softly, "If
I do, I shall want you very much."

She drew his head down; and kissed him . . .

And soon, they were lying close, a-quiver with desire.

And soon, they were lying still, desire past but warmth
and comfort with them and the memory of the hideous sight
outside almost gone. His left arm was beneath her neck,
cradling and his right hand gentled her soft skin. For a
while she could think only of the warmth and comfort, but
suddenly she thought: He's going to leave me, and she
drowsed off with that in her mind. Another thought stabbed;
a fear-thought, and she stiffened. Her lips parted but before

she could utter a word he closed·them with his; and when at last he drew them away, he said:

"Softly, darling; speak very softly."

So she said in a quivering whisper what she wanted desperately to shout:

"You can't escape. They'd stop you like they stopped Paul."

And in her mind's eye she could see the six men, striking and striking and striking again.

5

Escape . . . ?

"JANEY," PHILIP WHISPERED, "you saw what happened to Paul."

"Yes. That's why you can't —"

"That's why I must escape," he retorted. "This isn't a simple industrial consortium; this is something ugly, deadly, cold-blooded. The outside world *must* be told."

They were so close together and warm and snug. It was an age since she had lain like this, seeming as if in one way she had slipped back to the loveliest days of her marriage with Bruce. There was something else, a sense, an awareness, rather than knowledge. It was right to be here with Philip. No matter what had led up to it, no matter what his real purpose, they were one of another. It was as if she belonged to him, had suddenly become part of him. She was too tense in her mind and too relaxed in her body to think beyond that awareness, but one thing she did know.

She did not want him to leave her. The Project would be a dread and dreary place without him now. Yet as she allowed that thought to drift through her mind there was a companion thought, that this was absurd. How could she fall so desperately in love in a few hours?

His arm was firm and strong about her waist; he was holding her close and with the pressure of his body, comforting her and giving her reassurance.

"That's why you can't —" she had begun, the picture of that hideous attack on Paul vivid in her mind.

"That's why I must escape," he had interrupted.

Why had he said that? Why had he spoken as if she would understand?

Hazily, she *did* begin to understand.

"Janey," he whispered, "this is like a concentration camp."

She caught her breath: "No!"

He shifted his position slightly, making her aware of the lean strength of his body, the rippling power of the muscles in his stomach, in his legs. Now his cheek was against hers, his voice just reached her and she knew that he was trying desperately to make sure that no microphone picked up his words.

"It's happened too often before in modern history. When a man's nerve is broken, he disappears. If a man's soul rebels, he disappears. Only if he does what he is told, only if he asks no questions and meekly accepts the life he's allotted, can he live in peace and safety. That's true here. You must be aware of that by now. You of all people can't be blind."

But she had been blind, because she had wanted only to live in her world of personal sorrow and of grief.

There had been disappearances; there had been others from different departments who had shown signs of the same nervous tension as Paul; and vanished. She was aware of another thing: *not another man or woman had talked of this to her*. She, like everyone else, simply accepted the situation; why else could it be, but because they were afraid?

The fear was in Charles Leadbetter, in Freddie Ferris, and it had become naked in Paul Taylor. About them was a wall of silence. Despite the awful noise and the vibrations which never ceased, there was a conspiracy of silence. In all the time she had been here no one had talked about the conditions of their living, or anything except generalities, or music, the arts, the sciences. No word about working conditions, for instance, nor about the men who commanded them. Oh, in the common-room there would be fast and furious arguments about politics and about foreign affairs but these had long since lost their bite. It was as if they were living apart from the world.

A 'concentration' camp . . . ?

Philip whispered, "We can't let it go on without trying to escape so as to tell the outside world what's going on. Janey, everyone here is a slave."

"Don't," she whispered. "Don't go on."

"But you know it's true," he insisted.

"I don't — I don't want to think about it."

"Don't you?" he said in a queer voice. "Well, I haven't thought about anything else for a long time. Except —" he broke off, and eased away from her so that although they were still close from the waist down, she could see his face as he could see hers. His hands moved and his strong fingers played so gently with her, there was a curve at his lips and she had not realised before how strong and handsome he was. "Except you," he went on much more clearly, as if it no longer mattered whether he was heard. "Except you, Janey. *How I love you!*"

She thought, exultantly: How I love you!

But almost at once doubts crowded into her mind. He would say that to reassure her, he might even say that he loved her because of what had happened between them, but his motive both for loving and for saying that he loved her could be the same: to win her help in a bid for escape, the very thought of which she hated.

He kissed her, gently, and began to speak softly again: "We mustn't talk except in whispers."

She could not stop herself from retorting: "When we're in bed, you mean."

"When we're alone in the grounds, anywhere we think we're safe from being bugged. Janey, please — you *must* know that I have to escape."

One half of her mind already knew; the other half resented it bitterly and fought against it as if she were fighting death.

In the next few days she had long periods of bitter revolt, anger and resentment. When she was alone she thought, he *was* using her, cold-bloodedly, callously. But whenever they were together, in the restaurant or the theatre, holding hands in the cinema, dancing in the night club she had only been to occasionally before, she was quiveringly aware of him. And when he came to her at the day's end, and on the odd days off when they did not work, she was aware only of being in love.

Ashley looked up from a report he was reading as he sat in an armchair in his suite, which he shared with Parsons. It was midday. Even here, insulated against sound as well as the building could be, the muffled roar came, and the air seemed to throb, the floor vibrated in a way which some got used to but which drove others out of their minds.

"Have you read this latest report on Wylie and Carr?" he asked.

Parsons, who was changing records on a record-player, looked over his shoulder and remarked,

"It seems very satisfactory."

"It is," Ashley said. "I have only one reservation." As he said that his expression took on a sharp edge, giving him a predatory look.

"What's that?" asked Parsons. The record dropped and he moved across to an armchair opposite Ashley. His face reflected none of the smaller man's doubts, he looked completely self-assured as he lowered himself into his chair.

"It happened so quickly," Ashley said.

"Don't you mean it came to a head very quickly?" countered Parsons. "Carr must have been sexually aware of her for a long time."

"I wish I knew why it came to a head that particular night," said Ashley. He got up nervously, and went to a bookcase, selected a slim volume of verse, *The Rubaiyat of Omar Khayyam*, came back and sat down. But obviously he could not settle, and Parsons got out of his chair in turn, went to another corner of the room where a small cine-projector stood with a stiff cover over it. He took off the cover, pressed a button on the wall, and two shelves began to revolve until a small, silvered screen appeared in place of the books.

He placed some spools on the projector, a very simple task. All over The Project, in rooms, in the recreation halls, outside, in the laboratories, automatic cameras took pictures on tape which could be cleaned off and used afresh or processed on to film, as these had been.

"Come and see the lovers again," he said, indulgently. He pressed a switch and the projector whirred. Pictures of Janey and of Philip Carr appeared, sharp and clear and in startlingly natural colours. They were walking along the river bank, then across the lawns, hand-in-hand. There were pictures of them kissing, embracing, of them dancing cheek-to-cheek, eating, sleeping. Occasionally Jane Wylie seemed pensive but most of the time she seemed light-hearted and gay, while Philip Carr seemed to be more content than he had ever been at The Project, as if he had won his victory and asked for nothing more.

In the laboratories they did their work with much less preoccupations than before; and whenever they passed close or were standing together, they touched hands or touched bodies. From time to time their voices faded into a whisper, but always in moments of intimacy or embrace.

The film came to an end with a swift sequence of them lying close, in bed. As Parsons switched the projector off, Ashley remarked,

"I wish I knew what they whispered about."

"Sweet nothings." Parsons seemed completely convinced.

"I hope so," Ashley said. "I certainly hope so. We'll keep them under close surveillance for another week, until Taylor's replacement has had a few more days to settle down."

"We're still being watched," Philip whispered.

With a glint in her eyes, Janey retorted, "Perhaps we always will be."

"You'd be condemned to half-a-life here, even with me."

"If this is half a life," Janey said. "I've never lived at all before!"

They laughed, spontaneously. Everything they did and said indicated that they were becoming happier and happier, and except in flash moods of fear as to what would happen if Philip tried to escape, Janey was thoroughly happy.

Paul Taylor's replacement was an 'older' man, in his forties. Already mostly grey, he had a big bald spot, grizzled sideburns which were like mutton-chop whiskers, and he had a bushy moustache which had more of its original auburn colour than his hair. His pointed chin was clean-shaven and shiny. He was very broad but shorter than medium height, and he moved briskly although handicapped by some trouble in his left leg, which made him limp, and also made him turn towards the left with great care; either his hip joint moved more easily that way or he was in pain.

His name was Killinger — Eric Killinger. He spoke good English but with a foreign accent which it was hard to place. His specific job, as Paul's had been, was to test and analyse the oven and the synthetic materials from which the crystals were made, before passing the crystals to Janey who in turn prepared the containers for the ovens.

Occasionally Janey glanced over at him expecting to see Paul, and was suddenly overcome by what had happened, feeling a sharp pang of remorse that she could be so content. Yet she *was*. Philip seemed just as happy, and except for those flash moods of remorse and the stabs of fear about Philip's preparations for escape, she was untroubled. There were times when she asked herself whether she would be prepared to settle for this life for all time, and even though she always dismissed the thought, knowing that she would become homesick for the outside world, she was certainly prepared to live in this vacuum for a long, long time. Philip seemed to become more and more absorbed in their loving and their living. He still kept his own one-room apartment but spent most of his time with her. The nightmare of the attack on Paul had receded so that even when the mental image came it did not hurt; guilt quite died away.

Every now and again the noise ceased and brief spells of silence came, but they no longer brought shock. One struck as they were leaving the laboratory just before six o'clock, a later working day than most, for Leadbetter had come in from an interview with Ashley and Parsons and some other V.I.P. Ashley looked brighter than he had for a long time.

"We are getting nearer," he said exultantly. "There were pieces of lead which did not melt in some of yesterday's batches, Janey."

Her heart leapt.

"But that's wonderful!"

"It is indeed. And the whole of the team is to be congratulated and rewarded. We are to get a bonus of ten per cent on our salary, and the week after next, we shall have a longer break than usual from work."

Janey thought, a *holiday*? But no one asked whether they would be able to leave The Project area. There was excitement in all of them, particularly in Freddie Ferris, who had lost some of his nervousness during the past week.

They were going into the tunnel-passage when the noise stopped and the walls and the floor went utterly still. Killinger raised his hands in alarm; it was his first experience of the 'silence'. After missing a step, Philip tucked Janey's arm beneath his, and quickened his pace.

"Come on! I want every minute I can have with you!" He pressed her arm tightly; and in her room before she cooked a simple dinner, his embrace seemed to have an additional touch of passion. But it wasn't until afterwards that she suspected why.

"If we ever go out into the cold, cold, world, you'll be worth a job as a chef any day. I'd forgotten that mushrooms tasted so scrumptious and that minute steaks really melted in the mouth." And later: "Darling, I don't believe you did make this apple pie!" Soon, he put the *Suite from Swan Lake* on the record-player and stood over her as she sat in an armchair, content and a little over-fed. "Sweetheart," he said. "I've a report to make for the V.I.P.s, and I ought to go and do it. I'll be back by eleven. Will that be all right?"

"Of course," she answered. "It will give me a chance to do some chores." By 'chores' she meant some personal laundry and mending.

Instead of suspecting the truth, she was actually glad; work even in this tiny apartment did pile up.

She had to scurry to finish by ten to eleven, tidied up, and by a minute or two after eleven she was waiting. When another five minutes passed she was aware of their going, but not troubled.

After ten minutes, she wondered whether she ought to call Philip's flat, but all the telephones here were electronically controlled and if she showed any anxiety then the V.I.P.s would learn from one of the computers. She did not want to appear over anxious.

It was as that thought struck that fear followed, with a shattering blow. All contentment faded and she went cold. She began to shiver. *He wasn't coming back.* This was the night he had chosen to escape.

Oh, God! What could happen to him?

Oh, dear God, how could he leave her without a word of warning? How could he be so cruel?

She stood close to the windows, looking out, imagining figures in the shadows, moving forward as they had on Paul Taylor, but it *was* imagination. No one was outside. It was a wet and windy night, perhaps that was why he had chosen it.

How could he —

She stopped herself from these reproaches; if he had had to go then he could not possibly have warned her, lest she should show her emotions and warn all those who watched.

.At half-past eleven, there was no sign of him.

Nor by twelve.

She had not the slightest doubt now that he had made his attempt and wondered, anguished, whether he had been caught already, whether he really had a chance, did not help. She made herself her usual malt drink, then went to bed, acutely conscious that he wasn't with her; that he hadn't made the drink for her as he usually did. She was obsessed by fear, and was sure she would not sleep.

But she did sleep.

And she was still asleep next morning when Ashley and Parsons with two other men opened the door of her apartment with a pass key. The first awareness of waking was of a hand at her shoulder, shaking vigorously, and when at last she opened her eyes there was bright sunlight, and she knew that she was late.

Then Ashley asked in a cold, cruel voice: "Where is Carr? Where is he?" And after a pause he clutched her shoulders and his fingers bit into the flesh with sharp and intended pain. "You know. And if you don't tell us at once, we'll thrash the truth out of you."

She remembered the attack on Paul Taylor.

They took her out of her apartment to a small, barely furnished room, a strange room of mirrors. By the time she reached this room she was out of the shock, and knew that everything Philip had said about The Project was true. Philip's disappearance had shaken them so severely that they gave up all pretence. These were evil men. She would never be free from this place; might not even get out of this room alive.

A man she did not know asked in a cold voice, "Where is Carr?"

6

The Thunder

JANEY GASPED, "I don't know, I don't know!" And it was the simple truth. The awakening and all that had followed brought terror but the question, repeated, relief and elation, for Philip must have got away.

The man in front of her, not Ashley, not Parsons, had the thinnest lips and the thinnest face she had ever seen in a man. He had a long, hooked nose and hooded eyes and a high, domed forehead, the thin, grey hair receding. It was like looking at a man made-up to appear unearthly — inhuman.

"I do not believe you," he said in a thin, precise voice. "You were lovers too long for him to deceive you."

"He told me nothing," she cried. "Absolutely nothing!"

She was standing in front of the man who was behind a crescent-shaped desk; and she stood in a room of mirrors. She could see herself, naked to the waist, wearing only a white mini-skirt, which she wore for tennis. She could see her own reflection and the reflection of the man who stood behind her, holding a short whip in his right hand. There was no pretence about his disguise; he wore a white mask which covered his face, with slits for the eyes and the mouth.

It was very bright, glaring bright; and the lights all seemed to shine on her, as if to reveal her nakedness mercilessly. She was terrified with part of her mind but positively detached with the other. It was silent in here; there was no

sound but her breathing and their voices — and the soft
breathing of the man behind her.

The one at the desk looked at him; she saw this in the
mirror. And the man in the mask, the one who looked as the
executioner would before raising his dreadful axe, nodded
back. She saw this; she knew that the gestures and the
glances were intended to wear at her nerves, and she was
already close to screaming point.

The man at the desk nodded.

The man behind her raised the whip, and lashes seemed
to spray from it. She gasped, fought back fear but was the
more terrified. He flicked with his wrist and a dozen lashes
stung her, but there was no great pain; nothing she could
not bear. But what would she do if he really struck savagely?

Darkness, blackness, fell upon the room.

The silence was suddenly broken by what seemed a
thunderclap, but it was not simply one, or two, or even
three; where there had been silence there was this hideous
noise, assailing her like a physical thing — worse, far worse,
than the threatened lash. It was pitch black, and the thunder
did what seemed impossible, became louder and yet louder
until it filled her body and her head, seized her nerves and
tore at them until they were raw-red. She began to sway,
but as she moved one way hands pushed her back, when
she went off balance other hands pushed her; and this
happened again and again. Her head seemed to be severed
from her shoulders, it was as if the roaring was concentrated
inside her head and there was no bones, no brains, no eyes
or lips or nose or mouth, just this dreadful noise and the
constant pushing, and the awful agony of trying to breathe.

Suddenly, all went still and silent.

And as her body spun and her head seemed to be turned
to jelly and was one great ache, the lights flashed on.
At first they dazzled her, and made more pain but slowly
she was able to open them and see the man again, although
he seemed blurred and shapeless, too. And she saw herself,

and the man behind her, masked, perhaps the one who had been here before.

He held her wrists, behind her.

He held her so that her head was thrust back and her bosom forward.

The man at the desk said, "I shall not warn you again."

There was no strength in her body, her mouth seemed so dry that it could burn and her tongue clove to the roof. But she made herself gasp, "You've no right to do this to me. You've no right to — " She broke off as she felt a slight pressure behind her. Her arms were drawn still further back, and she thought the man was easing his grip on her wrists — oh, dear God, he was pinioning them with one big hand and holding the whip in the other.

"You have no rights here," a man said. "You will have no mercy, unless you tell the truth. *Where is Carr?*"

She gasped, "I don't know!"

Silence followed and as suddenly, another period of stygian darkness.

She could hear her own breath, rasping. She tried to brace herself against what agony would come next, and slowly became aware of dim lights, of pictures, of one picture thrown against a mirror and then reflected a dozen times. It was a man—oh, God, it was Paul Taylor, being clubbed, and clubbed and clubbed again.

Next, there was a woman.

Soon there were men and women, so beaten, so bruised, so broken, that they seemed like limp rag dolls, not the human beings they had once been nor the lovely body that she was. She tried to close her eyes but could not, the pictures flashed in horrible succession, first the living then the dead.

As suddenly as before all went still and quiet and dark. But soon lights appeared, and she could see the man at the desk and the darkened mirrors which gave little reflection. The man spoke gently.

"Janey," he said. "We don't want to do these things to you."

She made herself say, "You've no right to treat me —
anyone — like this. I'm just an employee, and — "

"Tell us what you know and what you were plotting, and
you need not worry," he promised her.

They had no right to treat her like this but she had no
power to prevent them. She had no doubt that what she had
suffered so far was nothing compared with what she could
suffer at their hands. It was no use talking about right,
all she could do was try to ease her own situation, and there
was only one way she could do that — by telling them a
little, enough to save herself but not to hurt Philip.

And Philip had escaped.

She gasped, "I don't know anything, I wasn't plotting.
All — " she caught her breath.

"Go on," the man urged, softly. "Go on, Janey."

"All I know is that he once talked about this being like
a prison, and of trying to escape."

"So he did? And how, without being overheard?"

"He — he told me when we were in bed together. But I
don't know where he planned to go, I tried to persuade him
not to try. I swear I did!"

"Why didn't you tell us before, Janey?"

"I — I love him," she managed to blurt out, aware of
his cold gaze. That made her hesitate for a long time before
repeating in a broken voice, "Because I love him so." And
then, belatedly, she went on, "Why *should* I tell you? I work
for you. I'm not a slave."

"Janey," the man said, "you should have spoken of this
talk of prison."

She was broken enough in spirit to say, "I know, I know."

"Then why *did* you keep silent?"

She said in an anguished voice, "Because I love him so."

There was silence. Soon, her fears flooded back and
reached an agonising crescendo when the man behind her
moved. But it was not to strike her. He released her wrist
and draped a wrap over her shoulders. She clutched it at
the neck to hide herself. At the same instant, a chair was

placed behind her and the man who had threatened violence and pain now helped her to sit down. Another man appeared, with a tall mug of coffee, hot but not too hot to sip. It poured warmth through her veins and eased her fear; and she began to tremble from reaction.

"I am inclined to believe you," the man conceded in his gentler voice. "But you know now what will happen to you if you are ever caught out in a lie. This is no ordinary place, but those who serve faithfully are treated well." He paused long enough to let the words sink in, with all their sinister implications, before going on, "We know that Philip Carr put a powerful sleeping powder into the malt bed-time drink you had last night. His fingerprints were found on the tin which contained it, and some of the drug was also found in his room." He paused again, and when he spoke next there was a steely note in his voice. "Now listen and watch with great care. I want to know whether you have ever seen the men whose photographs will soon appear; or whether he mentioned any of their names in your hearing — indeed whether you have ever heard the names before, from Philip Carr or anyone else." He paused again as she sipped, and the shivering passed: "Do you understand?"

Philip must have meant her to sleep soundly that night so as not to be worried because he was late. Or so that she could not reveal his activity and so raise the alarm!

"Yes," she said, "I understand." On the word the lights went low and another photograph appeared on the screen. But there was nothing horrific about this. It was the face of a pleasant-looking, rather wistful man, with a pale golden tan and silky fair hair, well-shaped lips which gave him a droll look. She had a vague feeling that the face was familiar, as a film star's might be; but she could not place him.

Someone she hadn't heard before said, "That is Palfrey. Dr. Stanislaus Alexander Palfrey." He pronounced the first syllable of the surname as if the 'a' were in fact an 'o' and

after a pause the man at the table pronounced it differently:
"Pal, as in pal, frey. Palfrey."

Suddenly, she knew who the man was. Her expression
changed and her eyes lit up as she exclaimed,

"I know who he is!"

"Who is he, then?"

"He's the leader of a kind of Secret Service."

"Kind of?" the other asked sharply.

"Yes. He — my husband was fascinated by him and often
talked about him. I remember now. Bruce used to say:
'Palfrey for Calamity'." Still excited, she stared even more
intently at the photograph, which was so good that the man
Palfrey seemed to be alive. "Whenever the country's been
threatened with calamity, the world for that matter, this
man Palfrey with his organisation has — "

She stopped, abruptly, drawing in her breath so sharply
that it hissed between her lips. Then, silence fell, utter and
complete. The picture faded from the mirror and the lights
went low. Gradually, her own breathing and that of the men
sounded, but seemed to add to the silence, not to break it.

At last, the man said, "Go on, Janey."

She closed her eyes, and said huskily, "Is The Project a
cal — " She checked herself and went on, "Does Palfrey
think The Project a calamity?"

"I have no doubt that he does," the man answered. "And
it would be, for him and for his out-worn concepts of
human society. What Palfrey and his friends, what the
governments of the world don't understand, is that today's
world *is* out-worn."

Across his words came another voice, one she hadn't
heard before; a deep and resonant voice which seemed to
come from about the man's head although no one was there.

"Stop there, Ramon."

The man with the lean features and the thin lips broke
off and said quickly,

"At once, sir."

"Show Miss Wylie the other photographs."

"At once," the man repeated; and he sounded as much in awe of the unseen speaker as Janey was.

There were moments of silence before another, remarkably handsome, face appeared, but one with which she was not familiar. Quietly, a name was uttered, broken into syllables: "An-drom-o-vitch." But it meant nothing to her. "*Stefan-An-drom-o-vitch*," the speaker intoned, and the name appeared on the mirror beneath the face. She was vaguely aware of having heard it before, and the fact that it was Russian suddenly reminded her.

"Isn't he a very big man? Palfrey's friend or — or — *deputy*," she burst out. "That's it! His deputy."

"You are quite right," Ramon said. "Did Carr ever mention him?"

"No."

"Or Palfrey?"

"I've told you — no."

"Or this woman?" asked Ramon, as the picture changed.

The woman whose head and shoulders appeared on the mirror looked to be in her mid-thirties, but she might be forty. She was attractive, in a particularly English way: soft looking and wholesome. She had dark hair, groomed rather formally, as if she had come from the same hairdresser as Barbara Castle, a Cabinet minister in Britain for so long. She had blue eyes and full, well-shaped lips, rather a short nose with a short upper lip. She wore a dress with a shallow V at the neck and although the photograph was cut above the breastline there was a hint of a full figure.

"Joyce Morgan," the announcer stated, and the name appeared beneath the picture.

"No," said Janey, with hardly a pause.

"Are you quite sure?" demanded Ramon.

"Yes, absolutely."

"Very well."

Other pictures appeared, other names were uttered and shown, but she recognised none. As she watched, she became aware of two things. First, that she liked all the faces, particularly Palfrey's, the Russian's whose name she could not recall properly, and the woman's, Joyce Morgan. Second, there were many non-English faces, one or two she placed from features as well as from names as French, Italian, German and Spanish; but there were many who might be from any country in the world.

At long, long last, the pictures were finished and a brighter light came on but not with the fierce brightness of the floodlights. Everything in the room seemed normal, she was now so used to the mirrors and the men.

The man who had been called Ramon, said: "If you recall any of these names, you must tell Mr. Ashley at once."

"I will," Janey promised. And immediately felt shame that she should be so eager to.

"And if you recall anything that Carr said you must report at once."

"I will," she assured him, mechanically.

"All right," he said. "You may go back to your apartment."

The man behind her came and helped her to her feet, then led her to one of the mirrors, which proved to be a door. She was very unsteady and could not have walked without his aid, and he did not seem surprised, for at the end of a long, narrow passage there was a hallway, and on one side, two wheelchairs with canvas backs and seats, invalid chairs. He helped her into one, and pushed her. She was so mortified that tears stung her eyes, and soon she was crying.

Suddenly, they stopped in front of an open lift, and he pushed her into it, followed, and pressed a button for the door to close, and the lift went slowly upwards. She had nothing with which to dry her eyes, until, still standing behind her, the man gave her a paper handkerchief. As she dried both cheeks and eyes, the lift stopped and the door opened. Only then did she realise that she was in the passage which led to her own apartment. He pushed her towards the

ooms and opened the door; once inside, he came to the
ront of the chair and helped her out.

He was still masked, as when he had held the lash.

He bowed from the waist, as if he were a servitor, not an
xecutioner.

He drew away and went out with the chair, and as the
door closed behind him she realised he had not uttered a
word, had been as silent as a dumb man would be.

Almost choking, she moved slowly, effortfully, to her
bedroom. The bed had been made and turned down, everything was exactly as she would expect to find it after coming
back from the laboratory. She was so physically exhausted
that she almost collapsed into bed, had hardly the strength
to draw the clothes over her. Yet her mind was alert enough
for her to realise how right Philip had been. This *was* a
prison — was a form of concentration camp.

Would she ever see him again?

Would she ever get out of here?

Had he escaped?

Her last waking thought was almost of exhilaration with
a sudden flash of realisation. Philip must surely have got
safely away or they would not have been so desperately
anxious for her to talk.

At last, she fell asleep; and slept, as she had grown ac-
customed to sleeping with the thunderous roaring in her
ears and the whole room, the whole building, roaring and
vibrating.

She did not dream.

When she woke, it was dark and silent.

She had a sense of movement but not of vibration, but
was too drowsy to worry about that.

When she woke again, it was pitch dark, but this time
she could not doze, so she got out of bed — and banged
against the wall, hurting her toe. Who on earth had moved
her bed? She groped for the light-switch on the bedside
table, but could not find it. As she groped about the room,

her heart began to thump with un-nameable fears. Even before she found a light-switch, set in the wall, she felt sure
she was not in the same room.

And she was not, for a single bulb shed a yellow light
about a room with pale green walls and metal furniture —
more like a cell or a hospital ward than the pleasant apartment she had lived in for so long.

BOOK II

The Fear

7

Move and Counter-Move

PHILIP CARR WALKED slowly along the platform at Euston
Station.

He heard people behind him and his body was tense, lest
one of these should attack him. There was something ominous
about the sharp clap-clap-clap-clap of metal tips, the faintly
squelching sound of rubber, even the firm impact of leather.
Men hurried; women hurried. There was the metallic rattle
of the tall hand-baggage carts on to which so many people
piled their suit-cases, and pushed. Two couples, arm in arm,
passed him; and one woman in her twenties was clutching
her companion as if afraid that he would run away.

As he, Philip Carr, had run away from Janey.

He gritted his teeth at the memory of her; and of leaving
her. There had been no other way, but how it hurt; and how
it must hurt her. But without the love affair, he would never
have lulled the leaders of The Project into a sense of security.
She would never know what value she had been to him: and
to so many others.

He wondered: is she safe?

He was as aware of her and his betrayal as he was of these
never-ending footsteps, as if with never-ending threat. A
woman came running. A porter caught up with him, pushing
a heavily laden truck, with tartan suit-cases and a heavy
leather trunk, as well as some attractive-looking pale green
luggage. He was a young-looking negro wearing the British

Rail uniform and Teutonic-type cap. As he passed he looked straight ahead but spoke out of the side of his mouth.

"You're okay, sir. The doctor's having you watched."

Carr's heart leapt, and the porter went on at the same steady but fast gait. The end of the platform drew near and the ramp where passengers had to go for the main hall and the taxis. A girl in the pale grey uniform of Mid-Eastern Airways came up to him; dark-haired, Jewish, with beautiful, olive-coloured skin.

"Excuse me, sir." She made him pause and also made him very wary. "Take an ordinary taxi to Number 1, Romain Square, Pimlico. The doctor will be there."

"Which doctor?" he asked.

"Palfrey," she said.

"That's fine," he responded, warmly, but he felt more wary still. There was still so much danger; but then, working with Palfrey was *all* danger. But it paid off! He now knew what Palfrey and others had suspected for some time, that The Project was much more than it had been — or appeared to be — when it had started. Then the consortium of industrialists seeking a way of creating nuclear power had seemed innocent enough. So had their insistence on absolute secrecy, their right to hire their own staff in terms of strictest confidence. The first anxiety had been when some had not returned after their first year's contract was over, although many — never from the research departments — had come home. Then, there was evidence found by Palfrey and his men, that letters were opened and resealed, an obvious form of censorship.

Enough of this thinking back!

Philip reached the huge, white-floored, white-ceilinged hall, with its bare austerity and the shops on either side, saw the sign: TELEPHONES and went towards it. He reached an empty booth, sat down and glanced round; the Jewish girl was not in sight and no-one appeared to be watching. He dialled a number which he knew off by heart and a woman's voice responded at once:

"Z5."

"Carr," he said. "Philip Carr. Number 107."

"Just one moment," the girl said. "Dr. Palfrey's expecting a call from you." The moment proved a long one — too long? Several people drew close to the telephones as if anxious to make a call, and from time to time each one of them looked at him; and each one, like the porter and the airline hostess, could be from The Project. Then he heard Palfrey's voice, clear and distinct yet gentle; a voice which could not possibly be mistaken.

"Hallo, Philip," he said. "It's good to know you're in London. You've nothing to worry about at the moment. The Jamaican porter and the Jewish air hostess are our people Do you see a man close to the telephone booth, holding a brown brief-case with Qantas and a T.W.A. label tied to the handle?"

There was such a man, in his early thirties, athletic-looking and of medium height.

"Yes," Philip answered, forcing his voice down low.

"He will follow you to Number 1, Romain Square, and I will be there to see you as soon as I possibly can. *Very* good to have you back," repeated Palfrey, and rang off.

Very slowly, and almost dizzy with relief, Philip put up the receiver and stepped out of the booth. A young girl with silky fair hair curling down to her shoulders and a black maxi coat reaching her ankles, pushed past him to get in. The man with the brief-case made a beeline for another booth which became empty, and Philip wondered how he could follow; but on such things he had never known Palfrey wrong. He walked down the stairs to the concrete caverns where taxis arrived, it seemed, from all directions. A dozen people waited, the young Jamaican porter was there with his truck-load of baggage.

Philip's taxi driver was also a Jamaican.

"Where to, sir?" he asked, making the 'sir' sound very like 'sah'.

"Number 1, Romain Square, Pimlico," answered Philip;

it must be like asking the man to find a needle in a haystack, and he wasn't surprised when the man asked, "Do you know where Romain Square is, sir?"

"I'm afraid I don't."

"Never mind, then; we'll find it." The taxi started off, and Philip sat back and watched the streaming traffic and the crowded pavements, the huge red buses and the heavy lorries. There was a heavy smell inside the cab, in fact everywhere, smell caused by smog of a million exhaust pipes which spewed their poison, and tens of thousands of factory chimneys.

And there was noise.

It struck at him when he pulled a window down, hoping vainly for fresh air, ear-shattering noise from a lorry and a bus and a heavy motor-cycle, — noise which made the streets shudder and vibrate, a constant roar almost as bad as the roar at The Project. Even when he pushed the window up, it wasn't much better. But he saw a car draw alongside in a traffic block at some control lights, and also recognised the driver as the man who had held the brief-case which Palfrey had described.

So from the moment he had stepped off the train, Palfrey's men and women had been watching him, probably while he had been on the train, too. He had caught it at Wolverhampton after catching a bus from a village called Sibley, which was about six miles from the 'prison' from which he had escaped. Before going into The Project he had learned the times of buses, and exactly where to go. He had telephoned Palfrey from an Automobile Association box, outside the village, spent the night in a small hotel near the station at Wolverhampton and caught the train which had arrived a few minutes late at Euston — at 1.52 p.m. It was amazing how quickly things had happened once he had escaped.

This same time must have seemed an age to Janey.

Especially if they had used torture to make her talk.

He tried to shut the vision of such torture out of his mind, and settled back in a corner. There were the good things, such as the evidence of Z5's concentration on him and on the problem. Palfrey's name was legendary, and everything Carr knew about the man was supporting evidence for that legend.

They reached Oxford Street, then Park Lane, bowled fast alongside the Park, the noise different now because of greater speed but still very loud. Hyde Park Corner was a mass of slow-moving traffic, and he looked across at the steel spike protection on top of the walls of Buckingham Palace, then out of the other window at the Quadriga statue, which, as with so many people, inevitably recalled that of Boadicea who had led the early Britons in the savage attacks against the occupying Romans. He thought of the cold, stone replicas of the knives fastened to the hubs of her chariot wheels as she had destroyed and plundered Londinium to avenge her Roman-ravaged daughters and restore the pride of her kingdom and the lands of kings, enemies before the Romans came, brief but passionate allies against the Roman legions.

Ever since there had been wars; as many waged today. And there was the war being waged between Palfrey's Z5 and the unknowns of The Project who poised a new threat at the heart of the world and its hard-won, blood-coated partial freedom.

What if men and women had to be sacrificed in these wars?

What if Janey had to be tortured, lacerated, mutilated, killed? What else could he have done but offer her as a sacrifice after such constant planning?

They were in the King's Road, with its boutiques and its flower-happy people and shops filled with gay clothes and boots and exotic spices and perfumes in the shadow of the wall of the Royal Chelsea Hospital, where the pensioners still lived out their lives, and on fine days came out and watched and must have marvelled at the long bare-looking legs and the inviting thighs and the sheep-and goat-skinned youths, the hippies, with hair as long as the hair of any of those old-time warriors.

"I seem to remember Romain Square now, sir," The driver turned his head as they paused at traffic lights.

"Good," Philip said — and sat back, and froze.

The man in a little blue car was just behind the taxi, and another man, whom he had seen among the guards at The Project, was in a car alongside him. In this car were two others, and one of them, next to the driver, had a radio-telephone microphone in his left hand, and was talking.

If they wanted to kill him, they could easily do so.

How had they been allowed to get so close? Why weren't Palfrey's men on the alert? Why——

He choked off his thoughts.

The taxi turned left, towards the river, to drive along the small and narrow streets, the houses where modern terraces stood close to tall Victorian dwellings and here and there a small but graceful Georgian house as well as tiny cottages which had stood in the same tiny gardens for at least three hundred years.

The car with the three men from The Project was close behind but there was no sign of the little blue car or of the man with the Quantas and T.W.A. labelled brief-case. Philip found his hands clenching and his teeth gritting.

Suddenly, men appeared from the nearby houses — not one or two, but dozens. One car pulled in front of the blue one, and on the instant the car behind him was surrounded. Before the occupants had time to lock the doors they were wrenched open, the men inside yanked out. Philip twisted round in his seat to see out of the back window, one of The Project men put his hand to his mouth, one of the invaders dragged his hand away. Philip saw the distortion of his face as whatever he had swallowed made him writhe and scream.

The taxi driver appeared to notice nothing, but turned two corners. A man wearing a peaked cap and a raincoat within an upturned collar, stepped out of a little blue-painted house which seemed to match the sky, and the driver asked in his soft voice:

"Can you tell me where Romain Square is, sir?"

"Why, yes," said the man. "First left, then first left again."
And he smiled.

Philip recognised him; it was Palfrey.

Number 1, Romain Square, was a Georgian house, the
walls painted white with black woodwork, black doors and
burnished brass knocker, letter-box and bell-push. There
were some smaller, pleasant houses on two sides of the
square, as well as a Victorian period public house with
weathered red-brick and bright-blue paint and a magnificent
inn sign of a seventeenth-century sailor in vivid colours, and
the name of the inn in letters in red: The River Smugglers.
The cab pulled close to the drive-way of the house, Philip
got out and asked:

"How much?"

"Sixty pence, sir, please."

Philip gave him a pound note, smiled quite normally,
giving no sign that he was so deeply preoccupied, waved
away the change, and went up to the front door. It had been
freshly painted. The cab drove off and the street seemed
deserted. As he stepped on to the small porch, the door
opened, and the tallest man he had ever seen stood there,
smiling, bending down a little so as to avoid the lintel.

He had a huge face with beautifully shaped features; many
had said he had the face of an angel. Now, there was an
expression of deep pleasure on it as he extended his huge
right hand.

"Stefan!" Philip exclaimed, and let his hand be taken,
although most men would fear that bones and fingers might
be crushed. Instead the big Russian's grip was firm but not
too heavy or too tight. He drew Philip in, then closed the
door.

One thing struck Philip above all else as the freshly
painted door caught the light, while closing.

In this house was silence.

The silence was disturbed only by their footsteps as they
walked up a curved, wooden staircase with a smooth banister

polished a deep red. There was carpet, muffling, but not killing the sound. At a square landing, Stefan Andromovitch turned into a room on the right. It was a drawing-room attractively furnished and well-kept. Out of one window Philip caught a glimpse of the river, deeper blue than the sky, and seen over aged and lichen-yellowed tiles which had once been red.

"Sap will be here in a few minutes," Stefan said. "Meanwhile would you like to wash and then have a drink?"

"I'll settle for a whisky and soda," said Philip, dropping into a chair with yellow velvet or velour covering.

Stefan poured his drink and a milder one for himself, passed it across and then sank down in the big couch, covered like the chair, which was just large enough; he would have overlapped most furniture, he was so big.

"Cheers," Philip said.

"To your very good health," toasted Stefan, "and very great success." He sipped. "You know you were followed, don't you?" When Philip nodded, he went on, "And we followed your followers. There were two groups, the three you saw and three others in a smaller car which approached from the other direction. They were communicating by radio-telephone, and we were listening in. No doubt they thought they had a wave-length we didn't know, but we discovered it some days ago. Occasionally they reported to a man they called Parsons; is that name familiar?"

"Yes," Philip said. "He is one of the lesser V.I.P.s."

"Yet not unimportant, I gather," Andromovitch said drily.

"The Project has an excellent communications system and many agents. It is clear, as Sap thought possible, that all main roads and all railway and bus terminals in London were kept under surveillance, and immediately you were found — as at Euston — agents were to trail you to wherever you went and then withdraw, leaving one man at every vantage point. No doubt they planned to raid us once they had our rendezvous. They may even think this the headquarters of Z5; it would be almost worthwhile letting them convince themselves!" The big man paused, only to go on, "But Sap thought it best to catch them all, so both car loads were taken prisoner, and he is seldom wrong."

Stefan Andromovitch paused again, his head on one side as if he were listening; then he heard a faint sound, leaned back and said,

"He's probably quite right this time, too. In any case, here he comes."

8

The Organisation: Z5

PALFREY APPEARED IN the doorway. He had shed his rain-coat and cap, and was remarkably like his photograph, but taller and thinner than Philip recollected from earlier meet-ings. He moved quickly and gracefully, gripped Philip's hand, then moved to the far end of Stefan's couch and sat on the arm. His grey eyes, with a haze of blue, had searching directness.

"Philip," he said, "we can't thank you enough."

Philip waved his hands, as if touched with embarrass-ment.

"It just came off, that's all."

"As I told you before you tried, we've sent four men to the Project before, and they all died."

"Yes," said Philip. "I know." He sat upright in his chair. "What I don't understand is why I wasn't prevented from reaching Euston, if I was followed."

"You weren't followed from The Project," Palfrey assured him, as Stefan had. "They watched Euston Station, one of the obvious places, and directly they started after you, we started after them. I can't be sure, but I think they let you live so that they could find out where you were going. They'd like nothing more than to wipe out Z5's head-quarters, that we do know." Palfrey stood up and went to the cabinet where the drinks were. "How's your glass?"

"Fine, thanks."

Palfrey poured himself what seemed a very weak whisky and soda, turned back and remarked,

"So they didn't drive you to drink!"

"Not quite," Philip said drily. "Talking of thanks — thank *you*. My cover from Euston was magnificent."

"You were watched from your hotel last night, at Wolverhampton Station and on the train," Palfrey told him. "That's how we're so sure you weren't followed from The Project." He resumed his position on the arm of Stefan's couch, and went on, "How did you escape?"

"I've been watching for a chance for weeks," Philip replied, "and I discovered that if any of the V.I.P.s or the trusted employees went away, they always went east along the river bank. I couldn't stay close enough to see exactly where they went but suspected a boat. There were one or two things which spoke for themselves, too." His lips turned down, and he looked droll and yet self-deprecating. "And they always came back from the same direction. The river is a stream which runs through the grounds of The Project, but it's been widened, and I don't know of any river in that area of the West Midlands."

Palfrey murmured understanding, and watched the other as closely as Stefan Andromovitch watched.

"I came to the conclusion that the route ran underground," went on Philip. "And I knew there was a yachting and boating-pool, a little marina, on the eastern fringe of the recreation grounds. So when I got away I simply followed the course of the river. There were only two guards," he added. "I watched when one of the V.I.P.s came away from the main concourse: one of the guards took him in a small motor-boat." Philip finished his drink and stood up and began to pace up and down. His voice sharpened and the speed of his utterance quickened, he sounded almost angry. "It didn't make a sound! I saw him start the engine and heard the ripple of the water but there was no engine noise at all. They seem to be able to muffle or insulate sound."

Stefan stirred, and spoke for the first time since Palfrey had arrived.

"Anyone who can control sound can control sound waves," Palfrey observed. "And while that could be invaluable as a cure for noise pollution, it could also conceal the sound of movements of big fleets of vehicles, or aircraft or ships. If an approaching army could muffle all sound of approach, then it could be very dangerous indeed. Or a flotilla of submarines or dreadnoughts — militarily, it could be devastating."

Almost reluctantly, Philip said, "I suppose it could be."

"In a hundred ways it could be," Stefan asserted. "The most sophisticated rockets fly ten times the speed of sound, so do a lot of aircraft, but the vast majority of ships and aircraft are still conventional. A war between Russia and China would depend more on its conventional weapons than the sophisticated ones. So would any war between small nations. In the wrong hands the power of creating silence could be very grave indeed."

Philip said abruptly: "And in the right hands a great boon. Well, they can certainly control it sometimes. I don't know exactly how except that it's through crystals which are being produced synthetically by the million: it could be that the crystals, almost weightless, are in themselves an insulation against sound." He stopped in the middle of a step and swung round so that he could see both of them; and his troubled face was vivid to them both. "But they're doing more: they're experimenting with the use of crystals as an insulation against heat and against radio-activity. I don't know how far they've succeeded. They've built up a screen of secrecy that's almost beyond belief. There must be twenty laboratories there. *Twenty*. The only one I went into was the one I worked myself. But now and again I was able to glance into others which were off the same passage as mine. And I saw a lot of waste outlets and some tell-tale marks left by the waste of crystals and ore and plastics. I saw the warehouses where the raw materials are kept, too — enough for fifty labs. the size of mine. And if that isn't enough," he added in a bitter voice, "I talked to dozens of research physicists there, several men very well-known by reputation. Every now and again a man I didn't know from Adam would drop a remark about the value of controlling or insulating sound. Most of them seemed to take it for granted that the purpose was benevolent, and secrecy vital in case any discovery got into the wrong hands. They were all dedicated. You don't have to be told a man's credentials — or a woman's, for that matter. As a breed, scientists of all kinds think in much the same way. Have the same reactions, use the same short-cuts in language. There's another thing: every conceivable kind of magazine and trade journal was kept in the common-room and reading rooms, and in the library. But those which disappeared to the apartments first, and those which got dog-eared from use, were the scientific journals. I tell you those people hunger and thirst for more news of the world of physics and chemical research. All of them. None dared say so openly, but I sensed the cold hand of fear on many of them. I wish to God I could have stayed longer, to find out more."

"If you had, you might never have discovered what you did, and we might not have found out for months," Palfrey said.

Philip spun round again and strode to the window and stared down into a beautifully kept, red-walled garden. He thrust his hands into his pockets to try to hide the fact that they were shaking so.

Palfrey and Stefan exchanged glances, but neither of them spoke and neither made any move to get up. Philip stayed at the window for what seemed a long time: two minutes, at least. When he turned to face them his expression was more controlled and his lips held the rather self-deprecatory curl which Janey knew so well. Still close to the window but with his back to it, he said,

"Sorry. I didn't realise what a strain it's been. But I'll get a grip on myself. If I talk it out of my system, I'll be better." Words spilled out again, very fast, so fast that they ran into each other and at moments were difficult to distinguish. "No doubt at all they are on the way to controlling sound. There would be as much din as in a dynamo shed, and it would stop suddenly although the vibration went on, the engines causing the noise didn't stop — only the noise. It happened fairly often, but no period of silence lasted for long, which suggested to me that they were trial periods." Abruptly, he asked, "Am I making sense?"

"Very good sense," Palfrey assured him.

"And there's more," Philip went on in a taut voice. "They guarded the synthetic crystals as if they were diamonds. None was ever allowed out of a laboratory. I simply dared not chance smuggling any out. But I *think* they are trying to insulate more than sound. I think some laboratories are trying to insulate radio-activity. Today we need lead chambers, heavy manipulators, reactors, built in such a way that it costs hundreds of thousands of pounds to seal off one generating plant. And even when we do it, we live in fear of a leakage, of contamination. If The Project does succeed in that, then that will be the biggest break-through in the history of power — of fuel. It will make coal as useless as sand, gas as archaic as candles, and the oil from the wells of the Middle East, South America and the U.S.A. about as much good as water from a poisoned well."

Half way through this diatribe he began to stride about again, driving his points home by stabbing his finger towards Palfrey, or thwacking one clenched fist into the palm of the other hand. Suddenly he stopped again, facing them, with his arms outstretched in desperate pleading.

"Won't these things be good?" he demanded. "Won't they lead to a world of plenty? Won't atomic fuel, cheap to make and easy to control, be what mankind's been waiting for since civilisation began?" He went closer to Andromovitch and now appeared to concentrate on him. "Answer me!" he cried. "Isn't that what man's been longing for?"

"Yes," the Russian answered, quietly. "And it is what Sap and I are looking for, all the time."

"Then why are we fighting the people who can provide it? Why do we have war with them, instead of peace?"

"Philip," Palfrey interposed, "we told you a little of what we knew and suspected, but not all. We knew that the research workers who were lured by big money to The Project must be working on these things. They could do exactly the good you say, if the knowledge was in the right hands. In the wrong hands it can be used to take over the military, industrial and economic life of a nation, even of the world. We had to find out what was really happening, and thanks to you we can be sure that by our standards, the standards of Western culture and civilisation, any secret process will be in the wrong hands. You can't possibly doubt that, can you? What would they have done to you had they stopped you from escaping?"

Philip didn't answer at once but great distress still showed in his manner. His arms dropped to his side, he moved towards the window as if he wanted to avoid the others' eyes, but he turned back again, helpless, now, and undoubtedly despairing.

"They would have battered me to death," he said, "or they would have put me on the rack, they would have torn at my very vitals to make me talk."

When he stopped, there was silence, stillness, too, for neither of the men on the couch moved; and neither seemed to breathe until Palfrey asked in a soft but steely voice,

"So how can you possibly doubt the use they will make of whatever they discover."

Philip, half closing his eyes, muttered: "Oh, I suppose I know it as well as you do."

"What is distressing you so much, Philip?" asked Stefan, standing up. At his full height he was enormous but there was such kindliness on his face, such understanding, that he caused no fear and aroused no anger. He stood in front of Philip, some six or seven feet away, and asked with

searching directness. "Did you leave behind you a woman
whom you loved?"

The colour drained from Philip's face. His eyes misted
over with tears as he fought to keep them back. Over his
head Stefan Andromovitch looked at Palfrey, who nodded,
sharing the Russian's sensitive intuition. He moved away.
Stefan put a hand on Philip's shoulder and felt the quivering
of his body, sensed the depth of his distress. Palfrey re-
appeared, wheeling a trolley, on which was hot soup, sand-
wiches with meat lapping over the sides, cheese and biscuits,
beer and coffee. He spoke as if there was no tension in
Philip, pushed small tables up to the couch and the chairs,
and ladled soup from a silver-plated tureen. Quite naturally,
Stefan and Palfrey began to eat, then Philip started, too
quickly at first but soon with growing relish. Palfrey opened
bottles of beer and poured out into tankards.

As he ate, Philip began to talk again until slowly the
whole story came out, everything about what had happened
between him and Janey.

"The astonishing thing is, I hardly noticed her at first,
but as I began to I knew how she could help and I hated
to use her. But it was no use, and — well, I've never felt
remotely like it about a woman. It was agony to come away
leaving her with those devils. And, just for a while I fooled
myself that we could work together. Now I know we can't,
and there's just one question in my mind: What will they
do to her?" And then between clenched teeth he seemed
to ask not the two men with him but the world: "*What
have I done to her*?"

"Philip," Palfrey said.

"I'm sorry. I shouldn't have burst out like that. A fine
Z5 man I've become."

"One of the best," Palfrey said gruffly.

"One of the very best, the rare ones," said Stefan.

Had they been different men he would have known that
they were simply trying to soothe him, but neither of these

would lie simply to place salve upon a raw and aching wound. They meant exactly what they said.

"And Philip," Palfrey went on. "You know she would have wanted you to do what you did, had she known the reason."

"I suppose so," muttered Philip. "But don't soft-soap me, Sap. It won't make me feel better. I had to betray her, I really had no choice, but that doesn't stop me from hating myself."

"If we can get her back, you'll stop hating yourself," said Palfrey.

Philip went very still. In the few seconds that followed it was as if his heart stopped beating and that he stopped breathing; and a new light glowed in his eyes, the helplessness faded. He gulped, and then asked hoarsely,

"You mean you think you can?"

"I mean I know we'll try."

"But how can you?" Philip cried.

"We have a much better chance now that we know we have to prevent them from going on, and also know a secret way in," said Palfrey. "And we've another chance, too." He poured out what was left of his beer and raised the pewter tankard. "Here's wishing Killinger luck," he said, and drank.

"Killinger?" gasped Philip. "Eric Killinger, the new man in Taylor's place?"

"Is one of our men," Palfrey told him. "And we have at least one other there. Oh, there's a chance for your Janey." He did not add that if she were rescued it would be a miracle. Philip would know that, once he had recovered from the ordeal of escaping.

Philip drained his tankard and put it down, he looked much younger than when he had paced the room — as if he really hoped.

"Thank God for that!" He fell silent for a while, and then stifled a great yawn and went on speaking over it. "Now I think I can really sleep tonight."

"Why wait for tonight?" asked Palfrey. "You'll be stay ing here for the time being, and there isn't a reason in the world why you shouldn't take a nap now." When Philip started to protest, he went on, "Try for half-an-hour. If you haven't dropped off to sleep by then, you can put a full report on to a tape, every tiny word or gesture you can remember."

"That's a deal," Philip agreed, stifling another yawn.

His room was a large one on the floor above, with an even better view over the walled garden. The ceiling was high and was beautifully ornamented, the huge bed had carved head and foot panels which might have been taken from an altar or some great fireplace. Next to it was a huge bathroom with a big bath which stood on splay-footed iron legs. The bath itself was flowered, in a great variety of colours, like the tiles of the surround, and the brass taps were so enormous that they seemed large enough to fill a Roman bath.

There were blue pyjamas.

"Ridiculous," he said as he got into them.

"Winston Churchill always got into pyjamas for his afternoon nap — or are you too young to remember him?" asked Palfrey.

"I can remember the legends," Philip retorted.

Once he was in bed he was warm and snug and comfortable. The fumes of sleep crept over him and he realised the simple truth: just as he had drugged Janey to sleep, so Palfrey had drugged him. Even the thought of Janey did not hurt; he was too tired to think.

But Palfrey wasn't too tired to think, and nor was Stefan Andromovitch.

"We need the whole area surrounded by troops as well as police," Palfrey said, "and we haven't an hour to spare. The only hope is to persuade the Prime Minister to give the orders at once. I'll go to Downing Street, Stefan. You get over to H.Q. and see Joyce, and get things moving there."

"Sap," Stefan said, "if there is a chance in a thousand, save Philip's woman. I beg you."

"As I see it, at best there's a chance in a million," Palfrey declared. "Preventing the V.I.P.s from getting away is absolute priority."

They stood and studied each other for a moment, two men who had been close friends for years, who were the leaders of Z5 — although one was a Russian citizen, subject to the Kremlin's laws, and Palfrey so very much an Englishman.

Without another word, Palfrey turned and hurried off.

9

Of Dr. Palfrey

DR. 'SAP' PALFREY was one of the best-known men in England, in the United Kingdom, some said, in the world. His name was synonymous with doom and disaster, yet also synonymous with hope; there was much fear of him and there was as much fear for him.

He was, in fact, a bundle of paradoxes.

He was the leader of the organisation known as Z5, and widely renowned because of his association with it; yet much of what he did and much of what Z5 did was highly confidential.

He had the trust of governments, from the extreme left, such as China, Russia and even little Albania; and from the right, including Portugal and Spain. Yet no single government — not even Britain's — could claim his whole allegiance, for his first loyalty was to the world. There could be no more characteristic nor more loyal Englishman, yet he saw himself as belonging to all nations, and his agents and his friends were drawn from every country and from many races, colours and religions. In fact his closest friend was the Russian Stefan Andromovitch, second in command of Z5.

It was years since these two men had met except at times of crisis, for the world's turbulence created crises of itself. But there were other dangers, threats to the world, which had nothing directly to do with the state of the world or of the hostilities between nations. During the time when Palfrey and Andromovitch had worked together in Z5 there had been many drastic changes in attitudes, in societies, and in science. Perhaps the greatest change had been in science; apart from putting men on the moon and so beginning the conquest of space and of the universe, there had been a whole series of scientific revolution. Once the greatest threat to international security had come from warlike nations set on conquest, led by such as Hitler. The might of a great nation had to be geared for such a war. Today, one man with a few assistants could hold in the palm of his right hand sufficient power to conquer and control the world.

It was against such men as these that Z5 was organised; against danger from the most unexpected places, and against danger presented in the most unexpected ways.

It was almost unbelievable how many men saw themselves as Messiahs, as God-inspired rulers of the world. And it was as unbelievable how many people, in small nations, in sects, in political groups, could be persuaded to believe in such Messiahs. Some were on the lunatic fringe, some could strike terror in one place or one small part of the world, such as the Mansons of Hollywood and Death Valley with their ritual murders, and there were some who could inspire burning faith in thousands of people in dozens of places.

Among these were genuine leaders of men, although many more charlatans. And among these charlatans, if Palfrey was right, were the leaders of the venture which, so far, he knew only as The Project.

He knew a little of this: more than he had yet allowed Philip Carr to know. Philip had done a remarkable job but in doing it had almost crucified himself, perhaps broken his nerve for all time. Sometimes, important Z5 agents underwent a period of emotional torment, and whenever he had reason to suspect this, Palfrey sent them off on a mission that paralleled a holiday, for they might not be able to do their job as objectively as they should. Any failure could be disastrous; so, it was essential never knowingly to take the slightest risk of failure.

One of the astounding facts that he had discovered was the extent of the hunger and thirst for freedom and for justice in men. Men who were virtually slaves, men who served these would-be rulers and these demi-gods would often risk their lives, risk torture, risk their families, to tell Z5 what was going on. So, word had come over a period of a year or more about The Project. First one man who had served out his year at The Project would telephone Z5 and report his uneasiness, for there was a number in the London Telephone Directory for the organisation, as well as a number for S. A. Palfrey; eventually another and another would call. Each told a little, but when all the pieces were added together the picture was ugly and alarming.

Some, Palfrey believed, were suspected by the V.I.P.s and killed in what appeared to be accidents.

One of the earliest men to telephone had used the phrase V.I.P.s, and it had stuck. He had actually called while working for The Project. This man had said,

"Take it from me, Mr. Palfrey, that place is like a flickin' concentration camp. Talk about forced labour! There must be five or six hundred of them who do what they're told or lose their hides for it ... The Project, they call it ... Then there's the professional class, see?" He actually pronounced the word 'perfessional'. "The chemists and scientists and the office wallahs, you know ... And then there's the V.I.P.s. One of them's called Ashley, he's a cold-blooded swine if ever I saw one. Another's Parsons he's not so bad ..."

When he had finished, every word being taped on a small recorder attached to Palfrey's telephone, Palfrey had asked:

"How did you manage to get to a telephone?"

"Had to drive one of the V.I.P.s — trusted, that's me! He's interviewing applicants for jobs in a village pub and I sneaked out to the telephone kiosk. I — strewth! Here he comes."

The line had gone dead.

Not long afterwards one of Palfrey's men had answered an advertisement for a research worker in crystallography, and been given the job, and had never been heard of again. A second agent managed one telephone call, listing names of some of the better known physicists at The Project, but before he had finished he had been cut off, and Palfrey had no idea where he had called from. He felt a tearing sense of urgency as he was driven from Chelsea towards Whitehall. He did not know Anthony Wetherall, the recently elected Prime Minister very well, although they had met when he had been Leader of the Opposition. Wetherall was that rare modern creature, a politician with an intellectual rather than an emotional approach. He would not be stampeded into helping, he would want cold facts.

The chief anxiety in Palfrey's mind was that he might take too long to decide.

A light showed in the back of the driver's seat. McMurray, the driver, was one of the oldest agents in Z5, where the casualty rate was high; he was still one of the best drivers, invaluable especially in traffic. Palfrey leaned closer to the greying, bullet-shaped head to pick up the receiver built into the back of the seat.

"Palfrey," he said.

"This is Joyce," said Joyce Morgan, his secretary and confidante for many years. She had recently married a man met in one of Palfrey's investigations, and was back only temporarily to help with this particular task. "Some results from questioning the prisoners caught in the cars, Sap."

"Ah. Good."

"Only one talked." went on Joyce. "He is an Italian named Mario Corelli with a criminal record, once involved in the bomb-throwing in Italy during some riots there. He is an extreme right-winger — the kind who used to follow Mussolini."

"Ah," breathed Palfrey.

"He has worked for The Project for three years, as pilot and chauffeur to V.I.P.s," Joyce went on.

"*Ah!*" exclaimed Palfrey again, and his heart leapt with fresh hope.

"He names Ashley and Parsons and also a man who gives them orders and who appears to be in command at The Project. The man is known as Ramon — just Ramon. He is always disguised when he leaves The Project area, wearing a false auburn-coloured beard and moustache. His voice is very metallic and resonant. When going in and out of The Project's plant he flies by a lift-off jet, they have three there, all used by V.I.P.s." That was something Philip hadn't known. "And Sap —"

Palfrey said, "Yes," but the word was drowned by the sudden roar of an engine close by him. McMurray shot the car forward, in case this was an attack, but it was a bareheaded youth with a pretty blonde beside him, obviously showing off. "*Yes,*" Palfrey repeated, more loudly.

"The V.I.P.s fly to another underground plant in France and one in Western Germany. Corelli has also flown them across the Atlantic but they are taken to their destination by conventional plane from a private airfield near Boston, and he doesn't know where they go."

Palfrey's teeth were gritting, as the full impact of this struck home — not one Project plant, but several. He had warned agents throughout the world to look out for such a plant but this was the first positive news that others existed.

"Go on," he said.

"The last thing might be the most important," Joyce said. "Philip Carr's escape caused something like panic. He thinks they are planning to leave The Project. Corelli and seven other men sent after him had orders to try to find his destination and to kill him before he entered any house or building. We got him only just in time." Joyce paused, and there was a change in the tone of her voice. "He said that Philip's girlfriend was taken immediately to what he calls the Torture Room, but he left before she had been put under any pressure. He does not think there is much hope for her."

"Keep that from Philip for the time being," ordered Palfrey.

"Of course."

"What made Correlli talk?" Palfrey asked. "Did we have to use much pressure?"

"Very little," Joyce answered. "He says that he couldn't stand the life there any longer, that he's been thinking of escaping for months, but all the aircraft and all the cars they use can be destroyed by remote control. He doesn't know why this one wasn't — when our men raided it, he expected the car and everyone in it and nearby to be blown up. It was probably because they hadn't the slightest indication that they were surrounded and the man in charge of the party didn't send out an alarm."

Palfrey wanted to ask, "Who is the man in charge?" but he stopped himself. There was now no shadow of doubt; they must try to raid The Project. They were driving along Birdcage Walk, with St. James's Park on one side looking fresh and colourful with huge beds of flowers, and the Guards' Museum on the other, so they were nearly at Downing Street; a policeman, warned by walkie-talkie was already holding up traffic so that McMurray could swing left, towards the Horse Guards. So he said,

"Call me at Number 10 if anything else comes in."

"I will," Joyce promised.

The car turned the corner, and then into the approach to the steps which led up to Downing Street. As it stopped, two policemen came forward, one to open the door, the other to escort Palfrey through the wrought-iron gate into Downing Street. A dozen or so people were standing opposite and several newspapermen stood about, cameras much in evidence. As Palfrey approached more policemen outside Number 10 itself, one newspaperman called out:

"There's Palfrey."

Another said clearly, "Z5 can't be involved in this!" And as he spoke, several cameras flashed. More flashed and the crowd surged forward as the plain, black-painted door was

opened, and a small dark-skinned man came hurrying out:
Palfrey recognised the Ambassador of one of the African
states recently involved with a neighbouring state over
mineral rights close to the frontier. This man turned towards
a car, waiting for him, then caught sight of Palfrey, and stood
still.

"Good morning, Excellency," Palfrey said.

"Good morning, Dr. Palfrey." The Ambassador's voice
was very deep and attractive; although a little overweight for
his medium height, he was an impressive looking man. "Are
you concerned with my country's problems?"

"Not to my knowledge," Palfrey assured him.

The other's face lit up with a vivid smile, a flash of very
white teeth.

"I am not sure whether to be pleased or sorry about that!"
He went to his car and Palfrey stepped into Number 10.

As he did so, there was a sharp change in the atmosphere;
subdued lights instead of bright day, soft carpets, a complete
lack of urgency. It was this air of leisureliness which impressed Palfrey most, for the last incumbent of Number 10
had infused a sense of haste, vigour, urgency, into everything
he did. An elderly man came forward, a familiar face; at
least Wetherall hadn't changed all the staff.

"Good morning, Dr. Palfrey."

"Good morning, Sill. Nice to see you again."

"Thank you, sir." Sill moved along the hall to the stairs.
"Please come up. Mr. Wetherall will see you at once."

So at least there would be no formal delays.

"Good," Palfrey said, and stood aside as Sill opened a
door at the head of the stairs, a room which Palfrey had
never entered on official business before. It was comparatively
small, and its one window overlooked Downing Street, so
it was very bright. One wall was lined with leather-bound
books, and most of the room was taken up with a large,
green leather-topped desk, two big armchairs and two coffee
tables. Two books were on a table close to the far chair, and
Palfrey had time to see that one was *Africa Wakes* by one

of the shrewdest London foreign correspondents, and the other was Gibbon's *Decline and Fall of the Roman Empire*, before Wetherall came in from a room which led from a corner.

Water was gurgling.

Wetherall was nearly as tall as Palfrey, a lean, austere-looking man with a silvery-coloured hair, cut rather short, a lined face with a healthy glow. He wore a dark suit which fitted perfectly on his square shoulders and flat stomach. His eyes, the lids wrinkled, the corners criss-crossed with tiny lines, were clear, bright-grey. His hand was cold, his grip firm.

"Good afternoon, Dr. Palfrey," he said, and motioned to the near armchair, the one farther from the books. "Do sit down." He himself sat down easily, hitching up his perfectly creased trousers. "I dislike starting an interview in the way that I must, but no matter how vital the cause of your visit, I have exactly sixteen minutes to devote to it. Will you have a drink? Brandy perhaps?" He put a white hand out towards the bottle casket and his fingers hovered.

"No thank you," Palfrey said, settling back in his chair. No two men could have looked less harried or hurried. "I have established that there is an extremely dangerous plant, mostly underground, where we permitted some experimental nuclear research by an industrial consortium. The plant is known to be experimenting, among other things, on nuclear power. It appears to use forced labour, with probably five or six hundred people working there, as well as some of our best physicists, who go on very high salaries." He paused in his slow and deliberate speech, as if to give Wetherall a chance to speak, but the Prime Minister sat silently relaxed and yet intent; his eyes, catching the window light, were very bright indeed. "I had much suspicion but no certainty of this, and managed to get some $Z5$ agents taken on as employees. Some died, in accidents which were probably murders, but one escaped from this place last night. It is probable that its leaders will attempt to leave the plant, some by rocket aircraft. It is equally possible that rather than allow anyone to take possession of it, the plant will be destroyed. Yet I think it vital — " Palfrey gave a deprecating little smile as he used the word — "to take possession of it quickly. What I would like, sir, is your immediate instruction to the police as well as the Air Force and the Army to take my orders to carry out a raid within the next hour or two."

He finished, and placed his hands on the arms of his chair.

It was quite impossible to judge how Wetherall was re-acting, for he sat as relaxed and still silent as ever.

10

Quick Decision

THE SILENCE SEEMED to last for a long time — interminably.
Palfrey retained his pose, even to a point of nonchalance,
but his heart was thumping. Minutes could make a difference;
an hour could make the difference between success and utter
failure. And with the time limit Wetherall had set, there was
no time for offering proof or for argument.

Quietly, the Prime Minister said: "Will you answer two
questions, Palfrey?"

"Of course."

"When did you know for certain that this emergency was
upon us?"

"Last night about eleven o'clock was the first positive in-
timation," Palfrey answered. "I knew the plant existed but
had not been able to locate the key places, because most of
it was underground. I'm still not absolutely sure, but I can
now show the general area the underground part is in but
there may have been extensive tunnelling and the key areas
may be miles from the place I know for certain. If there is
a map handy —"

"Tell me," interrupted Wetherall.

"It is within the area of Wolverhampton, Eccleshall and
Stafford," answered Palfrey. "I've already alerted the police
to barricade all roads in the area, and have asked for all
trains on all lines to be checked by my agents and the police.

I've also alerted the Royal Air Force and asked them to arrange for an umbrella over the whole area with reconnaissance flights at low level, and I've indicated certain objectives — such as a river, small industrial buildings, some apartment houses, and chemical waste in streams and canals. Further, I've asked the Army authorities to help the police place a cordon round the whole district, a cordon roughly seventy-five miles long. It can only be done with emergency plans — Lieutenant-Colonel Orbis, with whom I normally work, says that it is like asking to put plans against invasion by paratroops in hand. Too many different authorities are involved for me to cope, sir. But word from you to the various ministers involved would cut all the red tape."

"And many units are already poised?"

"Alerted, anyhow. The police are poised."

"Thank you." Wetherall stretched out for his brandy glass and sniffed, as if the bouquet would help to clear his head and help him think. "My second question, Palfrey. Are we in Great Britain to carry the whole cost of this operation?"

"The Z5 funds can meet a substantial proportion, sir."

Wetherall sipped, then put his glass down, and pressed a button. The door opened at once by an alert-looking young man with smooth, glossy, black hair.

"Sir?" He glanced quickly at Palfrey, then away.

"Get me in quick succession the Minister of Defence, the Home Secretary and the Minister of Transport."

"Yes, sir." The young man bobbed out, as Palfrey, feeling tremendous gratitude, got to his feet.

"I'm enormously relieved, sir," he said. "Thank you."

"Your reputation is such that I am sure you would not make such a request unless you were absolutely convinced the measures were essential. I shall give the necessary instructions and ask all the Ministers to make sure you have instant co-operation. And I will hold my breath until I hear the result," Wetherall finished drily.

"I'll keep in close touch," Palfrey promised, and as they

© Lorillard 1974

King Size
or Deluxe 100's.

KENT

WITH
THE FAMOUS MICRONITE FILTER

DELUXE LENGTH

If you have
a taste for quality,
you'll like the taste
of Kent.

Kings: 16 mg. "tar," 1.0 mg. nicotine;
100's: 18 mg. "tar," 1.2 mg. nicotine
av. per cigarette, FTC Report Mar. '74.

© Lorillard 19

Try the crisp, clean taste of Kent Menthol 100's.

The only Menthol with the famous Micronite filter.

went to the door, he asked with even more than his usual diffidence: "May I ask you a question?"

"Of course. I'll answer if I can."

"Oh, you can," Palfrey assured him. "If I'd said that Great Britain would have to bear all the cost, what would you have done?"

"Complained bitterly," answered the Prime Minister, "and probably recommended that part of the cost be deducted from our next annual contribution to Z5!" He paused at the door, and he put his fingers on the handle, but did not open it at once. "Palfrey," he said, "I don't know how long I shall be in office. We have a very slender majority and some of our own party members may defect. You are aware of that. I want you also to know that I am with you absolutely in your search for a world at peace — for world unity. And while I am in this position of authority you can rely on me for all the help I can possibly give you."

Palfrey, taken entirely by surprise, actually coloured, but his voice was very firm when he said, "That will give me and everyone in Z5 tremendous encouragement, sir. Thank you."

They shook hands; and he went out.

Once he was in the car again he picked up the radio-telephone which was on a wave-length used only by his headquarters and his agents, and when Joyce Morgan answered, he said:

"We're getting one hundred per cent support."

"Oh, thank goodness," Joyce said.

And in the background Stefan's voice sounded with a fervent "Thank God."

One after another, the operations began.

First, fighter planes and helicopters as well as reconnaissance planes of the Royal Air Force flew over the area, and photographs were taken by still and ciné-cameras.

Second, Army units and the Midlands Police barricaded all main roads and by-roads.

Third, police boarded all trains from main-line stations and carried out an identity check on each train — with some passengers protesting vigorously. On the Nuneaton to Euston run two men tried to escape from a train, were caught, and proved to have the haul from major jewel robberies from Birmingham in their luggage.

Just south of Warwick, a car tried to crash the barrier, over-turned and burst into flames. The police and soldiers dragged the two youths in the car clear, and found over twenty pounds of heroin in belts and waistcoats on their bodies; twenty times as much was consumed by the flames.

South of Coventry, a boy of no more than sixteen and a girl who looked much younger, scrambled out of a train and scrambled up a siding; when caught, they burst into tears. Both had fled from their homes to get married, without their parents' permission.

There were a dozen other little conspiracies, including a man of sixty eloping with a girl not yet eighteen.

But as far as they could tell there was not a single arrest of anyone involved in The Project. As the reports came through to Palfrey and Stefan in the London headquarters of Z5 it seemed as if the whole operation would prove a failure. No unusual movements were spotted from the air.

By half-past three troops and police had spread a cordon throughout the whole area, over meadowland, and uneven countryside, in woods, in villages, at small bridges over narrow streams, and began to close in. At vantage points on high land spotters were stationed, and it was virtually impossible for anyone to break through.

Palfrey, in the operations room at Z5, with a lighted relief map of England on the wall, saw the outline of the cordon, knew that it could not be broken in daylight, and turned wearily to Stefan Andromovitch. The large room was circular in shape, and maps of any part of the world could be projected on to the walls. Across one wall was an operations panel in front of which sat four operators, receiving messages from all over the world. At times, the four could be increased to ten, but this being a comparatively small operation, only four were needed.

At Number 1, Romain Square, Philip Carr slept.

Palfrey, called to his own rooms, an apartment built deep underground beneath the new luxury Elite Hotel in Piccadilly, opposite Green Park, flicked on the loudspeaker over which the call was relayed, then recognised the Prime Minister's voice.

"Have you had any results yet, Palfrey?"

"No, sir. None at all."

"Have you done everything you set out to do?"

"We've had the fullest co-operation," Palfrey reported. "The cordon is likely to be one hundred per cent effective in daylight, but groups from The Project could break out during darkness."

"Is there anything at all I can do?" asked Wetherall.

"Not at present, sir," Palfrey replied.

"Call on me at any time," said Wetherall, and rang off. That was at four forty-one.

At four forty-three, the observer in an R.A.F. helicopter sweeping along the length of a river which disappeared into some hills, going underground, saw several small motor-boats and a little pleasure marina in a place where the river had obviously been artificially widened to make a yachting basin. Within sight, close to the river bank, were some buildings which looked like well-situated homes and small apartment houses. On the sunny day, there was something idyllic about the scene.

"Probably a country club, with river facilities for fishing and boating. There are some outdoor swimming pools." The observer spoke into a microphone and the comments were passed on to the operations room at Midlands R.A.F. Headquarters. His voice was quiet and unflurried, holding a slight North Country accent. Suddenly, it rose, and he exclaimed, "My God!" There was a split-second's pause. His pilot turned to look at him, and he pointed downwards. Where there had appeared grass and meadows sweeping down to the river, six 'holes' appeared, and on the instant the observer and the pilot saw that the very earth was being rolled back. In each of the holes was an aircraft with folded wings. Each had jet engines. Each took off as the holes were still widening.

The observer, speechless for a moment began to speak on the radio again, when out of the blue a rocket came from one of the aircraft, too sudden for the pilot to take the slightest evasive action. There was a thud, as the rocket struck, and on the instant the helicopter disintegrated. Another, close enough to see the aircraft explode, drew closer still; and another rocket struck it, and the second craft burst into flames.

A third aircraft, flying much higher, took photographs and radioed to base, reporting everything as it happened. Only minutes later, Palfrey was listening to a replay on a tape taken by the Operations Room, with Stefan standing very still and listening, other agents in the doorways or at their desks, mesmerised by the news.

The record went on, the pilot's voice touched with excitement as he said,

"All six aircraft are now at about eight thousand feet, flying west . . . They are bloody fast." There was another pause before he went on: "Six more are coming out of the open sites . . . They're in vertical take-off jets which straighten out and start flying at about four thousand feet. My *God*. There are six more . . . All flying west, but the first six are out of sight, they must be flying at a thousand miles an hour . . . There don't seem to be any more."

At that moment he drew in a hissing breath.

And at that moment, down on earth, villagers and people in small towns heard crash after crash as the aircraft from The Project broke the sound-barrier. Experienced pilots and other air crews who saw them from the ground marvelled at their speed.

All the booms had faded, the skies were clear except for the the reconnaissance aircraft, conventional and helicopters, when there came another boom. This was frighteningly louder, and a series of explosions followed, each as loud. Horses and cows and sheep stampeded. People rushed out of doors as windows shattered, mothers clutching frightened children, old people struggling to get downstairs or out of doors. Within the cordon flung round The Project by Palfrey, cottages and houses collapsed with the blast, sheds were hurled hundreds of feet into the air, people were thrown about like feathers.

One village, which had been standing calm and peaceful for five hundred years, collapsed literally like a pack of cards. One cottage crumpled on to another and added its weight to the effect of the blast which had already weakened the roofs and walls. All over the area similar disasters struck. It was as if the whole district had suffered an earthquake the effect of which spread wider and wider. It seemed an age before silence fell.

At Z5, Palfrey and Stefan listened, taut-faced, to the relay of the pilot's report. The hissing breath had been the only sound for several seconds, Palfrey waited for the explosion which he thought bound to follow, convinced that the aircraft had been hit. Instead, the observer began to speak again but in a strained voice. He used short sentences, as if he couldn't hold breath long enough to string more than a few words together.

"It's — unbelievable... The whole earth's rising... Huge buildings are — collapsing. Great holes are appearing... buildings are falling into them... The river — the river's disappeared... Now there's smoke — and flame!... Everything's burning, the whole of the earth down there seems to be burning... There's another explosion... And another... There must have been a whole arsenal... And — and houses miles away are — are collapsing... The very earth seems to be caving in ... And the fire's white hot... White hot."

Palfrey moved slowly away from the Operations Room, beckoning Joyce, who seemed unable to hurry. Stefan stayed where he was. Palfrey turned into his own office and lifted a telephone. "Get me the Prime Minister," he said, and as he waited, looked at Joyce, dark-haired, pale-faced Joyce Morgan. "We want a transcript of that report sent to all our headquarters and main agents," he said. "At once." She looked at him for a moment with great compassion, for he was like a man struck with horror. Then, she turned away. "I don't care where he is, he must be interrupted." Palfrey went on with restrained savagery in his voice. As he waited, his right hand strayed to his hair and he began to twist a few strands round his finger. He stopped when he heard Wetherall's voice, and spoke with great precision. "The whole area around The Project has been blown up, sir. Virtually disintegrated. The full extent of the damage isn't yet known but the force of the explosion was very great indeed . . . My chief concern is that it is probably an underground nuclear explosion. If it is, the whole area is contaminated by radioactive dust. With the wind from the west, the dust could be over the big Midland cities at any time. Birmingham, Coventry, Wolverhampton —"

The Prime Minister interrupted.

"I can see the urgency, Palfrey. If anything can be done we will get it done."

I I

The Green Clouds

THE WIND FROM the west carried the radio-active dust slowly towards the great Midland cities, to the huge car factories and the engineering works, to the main plants of every kind of product from cheap beads and costume jewellery to glass, to steel, to massive machines which, when transported by road, had a police escort because they were so huge.

People saw the cloud; it was like a pall.

Military observers saw it, too, and traced its path, and watched the places where it drifted low, first over the fields and the browsing cattle, then touching the roofs of timbered cottages, the spires of ancient churches, the highways.

There were no other outward signs of disaster.

Palfrey, in the operations room at Z5 headquarters, watched the scene on television relayed from a Royal Air Force reconnaissance aircraft, and listened to the commentary which was channelled through an R.A.F. base. Reports from different centres and different villages and towns integrated so he, Palfrey, and dozens of others in different places of vantage, could understand the general picture.

Except in the immediate area of devastation, still covered by a cloud of greyish-white smoke, there was nothing but the surprise and interest created by the cloud. Those places which had been shattered by the blast looked, already, as if they were derelict. Ambulances crawled through the rubble-littered streets and highways, but found few signs of life. Villages lay waste, too. But overall pictures of the scene showed how the damaged area was restricted; it was contained within a circular area ten miles across, with the main damage, presumably The Project, in the centre. Beyond the perimeter there was some glass damage, broken windows, slates and thatch off roofs, and sheds, fences and greenhouses down; but here the people seemed unhurt, more bemused than frightened.

One television reporter visited a small town, inviting comments from the people.

"*It must have been a tornado,*" was a common guess.

"*It could have been an army dump blown up.*"

"*It was much louder than an ordinary bomb.*"

"*It was like an earthquake!*"

"*It was like a nuclear explosion . . .*"

The scene switched to the sky and drifting cloud, and Palfrey saw the fear on the faces of the people; fear heightened when an attractive girl, her long shapely legs exposed by a brief mini-skirt, said very slowly,

"*The clouds are turning green.*"

And they were.

As the camera focused on the heart of the clouds a faintly luminous green showed, as if the sun itself had turned green and was bombarding the sky with tiny particles of fluorescence. The colour-shade remained the same but grew deeper. There was no green on the houses or in the clear sky, only reflected from the drifting smoke.

Now, people in the cities noticed it. The cameras swept over them and Palfrey and Andromovitch watched the upturned faces. Around the statue of Lady Godiva in Coventry, from the shell of the bombed old cathedral and the steps of the new one built in such hope, people stared and pointed; and as the close-up pictures were shown, fear touched many more faces, and the green was reflected in a thousand eyes.

Near the great new Bull Ring area at Birmingham, it was the same.

At Warwick and Kenilworth, too, the green haze shone on sightseers within the castle walls, and at Stratford-upon-Avon on the windows of the timbered houses and the tourist-crammed streets, and as the camera moved it became obvious that while there was some reflection, most of the green was actual dust, falling on the buildings as well as on the heads and bodies of the people.

In Z5 headquarters, Stefan said huskily, "If that dust is radio-active, the disaster is unparalleled."

Palfrey nodded, saying, "There's no confirmation, yet."

"It must have fallen on millions of people," Joyce Morgan observed. She moved from the corner of a desk and drew closer to Palfrey. "How long does it take for the symptoms of radio-active contamination to show?"

"A few might die quickly," Palfrey answered. "Nearly everyone who gets a powerful dose of gamma rays will be incapacitated within a few hours."

"If that is over eight hundred rontgens, then nearly everyone who gets the dose will die within six weeks. With smaller doses death can take a long time to come." Stefan spoke in a voice which revealed his horror. "Leukaemia and cancer may not show themselves for a long time."

For a few moments there was silence in the Operations Room; everyone in there was touched by the same horror as Palfrey and Stefan. A light glowed at a telephone near Palfrey, and he picked up the receiver.

"Palfrey," he said.

"Individuals are being taken at random from the affected places," a man at the central Control Panel told him. "Radio-activity is in the centre of the damaged area but none appears to have fallen yet. The people are being checked and tested. The first reports should come within the hour."

"Good," Palfrey said. "I'll be in my office." He put the telephone down sharply, and stood up. "Time we made a move," he said over his shoulder, and the others followed him, Andromovitch towering over Joyce, although she was not small for a woman. Palfrey held the door of his office open for them and then went across to a crescent-shaped desk. Behind him on the wall was a projection of the world so that the hemispheres and the main continents were shown. Here he could receive messages from Z5 agents everywhere, and could also send messages to all agents. The main control was in the Operations Room, this was a kind of extension of that.

Palfrey said, "Should you telephone Moscow, Stefan?"

"Yes, at once."

"I'll take Washington first, you take Moscow," said Palfrey. "All we need give them are brief reports. Joyce, love — while I'm talking to Washington will you take it down? We'll use it as a basis for a general call."

Joyce came to the desk, with a notebook and ball-point pen, and at the same time switched on a tape-recorder attached to the telephone. Palfrey leaned forward and pressed a button, and a tiny green light showed on the spot where Washington appeared on the map. Almost at once he was talking to Jonathan Keller, Z5's chief agent in Washington, whose office was only a hundred yards from the White House.

"Jonathan," Palfrey said. "There's a red alert."

"I was afraid this call might mean trouble," said Keller. "The Pentagon was on to me only ten minutes ago asking if I knew anything about a nuclear blast in Britain. Have you had a major disaster?"

"We don't know for certain what it is," Palfrey replied. "We do know that there was an explosion below ground at The Project. We've some reason to believe there are other Projects in the United States and elsewhere. We also know that eighteen silver-grey vertical take-off jets left the area before the explosion, and some might be headed your way. There's at least a chance they could change colour *en route*, so anything unusual wants watching closely. Can you have an alert at every airport, and from as many possible landing places as practicable?"

"Yes, of course," Keller said.

"Fine. Call me if there's word."

"Yes," Keller said again. "Sap —"

"Well?"

"Is the radio-active dust over your Midlands area?"

"In places, yes."

"Then millions might be contaminated already," Keller caught his breath.

"We'll soon find out," replied Palfrey, grimly. He put down the receiver, and immediately pressed for his chief agent in Calcutta, and gave the report. By the time he had finished, Joyce pushed a slip of paper in front of him. It read:

Suggested red alert to each divisional headquarters and all senior agents, to read: "Refer all previous reports related to The Project. Stop. Eighteen vertical take-off jets coloured silver-grey without marking left The Project in Midland area of England around 4.40 p.m. Keep close watch for arrival of any such aircraft or any strange and unidentified aircraft and trace to final destination which may be another major or possibly a secondary Project. Stop. Immediately after take-off a major subterranean explosion occurred and caused extreme damage up to five miles from the explosion source. Explosion could be nuclear leading to severe radio-active fall-out over a conurbation covering millions of people. Stop. Your military authorities and all who are connected with the treatment of such fall-out should be alerted at once since there could be other explosions. Stop. Radio-active dust could by now have reached Manchester and London airports and jet trans-atlantic aircraft as well as aircraft to all parts of the world could be contaminated. All arriving from London Heathrow or Ringwood Manchester should be quarantined and checked."

Palfrey read this slowly, transposed the word 'jet' so that it followed the word 'transatlantic' put the word 'secretly' after the word 'trace' and then handed it back. Joyce went immediately to the Operations Room, and within seconds the message was going out to thousands of agents. By the time Palfrey had finished Stefan came off the Moscow call.

"Problems?" Palfrey asked.

"They want to know if we have any reason to believe there is a Project in Russia," Stefan replied. He was smiling faintly and that curious saint-like expression was more marked than ever. "Sap, these crises have one good effect: they give all the big nations a common cause."

"Through common fears," said Palfrey drily. "Is that so good?" He began to play with a few strands of hair again as he went on: "If this dust *is* fully radio-active, then —" he broke off, as if he could not face the simple truth.

"Then a huge area of Britain will be wiped out," Stefan observed in a curiously flat voice.

"If not more," Palfrey said in an expressionless voice. He moved to a television set and was immediately switched on to a scene in Coventry. A small ambulance was in the main square, and a woman with two children, one in a pushchair, one standing by it, was looking down at the child in the pram. She looked shocked.

"He — he's turning green," she said hoarsely. "He —" then she looked up into a sky coloured green, instead of pale blue.

Palfrey said gruffly: "I must talk to Philip," and lifted the telephone.

Her name was Adamson — Gloria Adamson.

She was a sunny-natured woman, and much much happier than most. She was married to a shop-steward at one of the big car factories, and still in love with him. She had the two children: George, named after her husband, and Lucy, named after her mother. In a welfare society she needed nothing and even had money over for extras and special pleasures. Since her marriage, seven years ago, she had known no great tragedy or unhappiness, and she suffered less than most mothers from the problems of baby and child care because both the children had her own even temperament. Except when teething or when physically hurt, George had seldom cried and Lucy had only occasional fits of crying.

Now, Gloria Adamson was scared.

"He — he's turning green," she said, and looked up towards the sky.

It was green, too.

An ambulance drew up alongside her, and she noticed it but was still marvelling — awestruck. Other people nearby had a dusting of green on their clothes and even on their hands and faces. The driver of the ambulance and one attendant came from the car, wearing shiny-looking suits which might be of white oilskin, and masks; gas masks.

Gloria Adamson gasped: "It's gas!"

"No need to worry," the driver reassured her. "But we'll get you to the hospital quickly." He helped them in, the other man lifted the pushchair in beside them, and almost at once the ambulance was driven off, tyres going over a faint green powdering of dust.

"It's like green snow," a man remarked.

"I heard that woman say it was *gas*."

Another woman cried out: "Is it-poisonous? Is it?"

"Mummy, don't —" a child with her began.

"It is, it's poison gas!" the woman gasped.

An old man said in a quavering voice: "It's phosgene, that's what it is. A killer. Phosgene's green."

Almost on the instant there was a rush for the shops, and in a few seconds the rush became a stampede. Men and women were pushing each other, two children fell and were trampled under-foot, their mothers screaming as they tried in vain to help them. The words: "Poison gas — phosgene — a killer; poison gas — phosgene — a killer," floated above the heads of the crowds as the green dust floated gently down.

"Philip," Palfrey said into the telephone, "are you sure there was radio-activity at The Project?"

"Of course I'm sure," Philip answered. "It was undoubtedly the main source of power."

"There couldn't be any mistake?"

"Not the slightest chance. Why —" Philip broke off, and in a moment his voice rose. "What's happened?"

Palfrey hesitated, but only for a moment. Philip had to be told sooner or later, and delay might make him feel even worse about Jane Wylie. So Palfrey said,

"They've blown the place up."

"They've done —" Philip broke off again, and after what seemed a long time, he breathed, "Oh, God. Janey!"

"No shadow of doubt," one of the research workers close to the great hole where The Project had been. "It is radio-active. We must warn the V.I.P.s."

The geiger counters rattled away as if they were trying to cackle a warning to the men who used them.

12

The Tests

GLORIA ADAMSON STOOD in a small room, naked, with a peculiar glow shining on her from all sides and from the ceiling. It was like having a shower without water. There was a big square of glass in one wall and she could see the children, sitting in chairs which were too big for them. George was eating a bar of chocolate, so he was happy; and Lucy had an ice-lollypop in her left hand and the red water-ice was smeared over all her lips and chin, *she* couldn't be happier. Two nurses and a young, coloured doctor were with her.

No-one was with Gloria.

She stood as still as she could, fidgeting a little, feeling as if she were being watched all the time. She had her arms folded in front of her, shielding her breasts. At one place on her hip there were the shimmery stretch marks on the skin which had come after she had carried George.

Suddenly, a man said as if he were inside the room: "All right, Mrs. Adamson, thank you. If you'll open the door you'll find a dressing-gown behind it. Put that on and then come through the shower room — we want to wash everything off you — wash your hair as well, if you will, and use plenty of soap. Then come through the second door."

"*Am I all right?*" she cried.

The man appeared not to hear her.

She was trembling as she did what she was told. The shower was pleasant and she soaped herself freely, then rinsed and dried, but once that was over she slid her arms into the voluminous white towelling dressing-gown, and began to shiver. When she opened the second door she was in the surgery of the doctor she had seen just before coming in here, but this man was different; tall, slim, nice-looking.

"You've got to tell me!" she cried. "Are my children all right?"

The man said reassuringly, "As far as we can judge, yes."

"Was it gas?" she cried.

"Mrs. Adamson," the man said, "we aren't yet sure. But it wasn't one of the conventional gases, I can assure you of that. I am in charge, my name is Dr. Palfrey, so I would be the first to know."

"It won't matter whether it was conventional or not if it kills me or my children," Gloria said. Dressed in white with the collar tight about her neck and her dark hair curly and dishevelled, she looked most attractive, and her eyes glowed bright as glass. "I want to know what it was."

"As soon as we know for certain we'll tell you."

"I want to know what you think it might be!"

Dr. Palfrey did not answer, but a change came over him, and his expression softened. He stretched out his hand in a kind of appeal, and then said huskily, and very slowly,

"Are you sure you want to know?"

"Yes, I do."

"All right," he said. "We think it possible that you and your children have come in contact with radio-activity. There have been traces here and there, although radiation does not appear to be everywhere in the dust. We are applying all known tests, to try to make sure, and we are using all known cleansing and decontamination methods."

She seemed to recoil.

"There was an accident at a nuclear power station," he told her, and that was as near the truth as anything could be. "I promise you that we are doing everything we possibly can."

She seemed to choke.

"You mean — that green dust was radio-active?"

"Parts were. All of it could have been, but there are some most encouraging signs," the doctor replied.

"Oh, my God," she moaned. "My children."

"We've done everything —" the doctor began, but she silenced him by an imperious wave of her hand, and with something more — her expression. She was not beautiful, and until this moment he had not even thought her striking-looking or attractive. She took on some quality which he hadn't noticed before, as she said,

"But there were *thousands*."

"Thousands of what?" he asked, as if puzzled.

"People," she said.

"You mean in Leofric Square?"

"Everywhere — everywhere the green dust fell."

"I know," the doctor said.

"Who's helping *them*?"

Dr Palfrey moved towards her with a hand outstretched, and this time she did not back away. His face was very close to hers, now, she saw the delicacy of his features, sensed his understanding and compassion. He did not actually touch her as he said,

"They are going through the cleansing stations as fast as we can get them through: civil defence is really in action. And the streets and houses are being washed with a newly discovered decontaminating agent as fast as it can be done. Meanwhile, you are being a great help, Mrs. Adamson."

"But *I* can't help them!" she cried.

"Yes you can," insisted the doctor, and for the first time she felt that she had seen and heard him before. "We are checking your skin — your blood, your saliva, your urine, everything which might indicate whether you have been contaminated. Every modern test has been applied both to you and your children. If you and your children are free from contamination then everyone else is free from it. And once the people know that, it will be a great help, because there is much fear and despair abroad."

She put out her hand, in turn, and touched his gloved

hand. He did not shrink away, for fear of contagion; he seemed completely at ease, and so put her at her ease.

"But how will that help?" She wanted to know.

"I want you to go on television," Palfrey said quietly. "I want you to be interviewed and I want you to be photographed undergoing all the tests you've already done, and others in addition. And I want to tell everybody in England that you are —"

"A guinea-pig," she exclaimed.

Palfrey laughed, "In a way. You'll be wonderful for their morale if you will just be yourself."

"I expect I'll be terribly self-conscious," she remarked.

"Will it help to know that you've been televised since you stepped into the ambulance?" asked Palfrey. "What we've just said is on tape and can be broadcast with the picture."

She threw up her hands, and exclaimed, "*You devil!*"

Palfrey laughed again, and asked mildly,

"May we show the pictures?"

"But I was in the altogether!"

"And a very nice altogether, too," rejoined Palfrey. "Mrs. Adamson, what we need is someone to behave naturally, like you do, to show fear at times but not to be terrified or hysterical. The country has suffered what might be a devastating blow and if the worst comes to the worst — well, few of us will live much longer. But there are some encouraging signs. You and your children came through the skin test very well — there are no signs of radiation damage. And the geiger counter — do you know what a geiger counter is?"

"Of course I do," she retorted. "Do you think I'm daft?"

Palfrey chuckled. "If you're daft, the rest of the world is absolutely crazy! I —" there was a faint buzzing sound behind him, and although he didn't look round, he stood up. "Just stay there and watch and listen, please," he said, and went to the door and then pressed a button.

A man said, "We've found Jimmy Adamson, Sap."

"What did he say?" gasped Gloria.

"Is he with you, Stefan?" asked Palfrey.

"No, but he's on the telephone."

"Have you put him in the picture?"

"Yes. He would like to talk to his wife."

"Put him through to me, first," Palfrey asked, and he beckoned with his free hand to Gloria, who came hurrying, tripped over the loose belt of the towelling robe, fell, and grabbed at Palfrey to save herself. In that moment she seemed to be clinging to a lover.

A man said, "This is Jim Adamson," in a strong north-country accent.

"Jimmy!" cried Gloria.

"Mr. Adamson," Palfrey said, easing her away from him. "Your wife has undergone a number of examinations includ-ing one in which she was bathed, while completely unclad, in a ray which is a new and very stringent test for radio-active contamination of the skin. We would like to broadcast the pictures on television because we think they will show all other people who might be affected that every con-ceivable check has been made. If they can be positively as-sured by morning that all the tests have proved negative, they will be greatly reassured."

There was a short pause before the man spoke again.

"Why did you have to choose my wife, can you tell me that?"

"She was available at exactly the time a Civil Defence unit in Coventry was ready to make the tests. May we go ahead?" Palfrey's left arm was bent, the telephone in his hand, the other arm was round Gloria's shoulder, restraining her from grabbing the telephone. "May we —"

"I want to talk to her myself," Jimmy Adamson declared.

"She's standing by me," Palfrey said, and let her go at last.

The odd thing was that when she had the telephone in her hand she was very quiet, and when at last she said, "It's me, Jimmy," her voice was hardly audible. But Adamson's was brisk and clear.

"Do you know what they want to do, lass?"

"Yes, dear," she answered.

"Don't let them make you do it if you don't want to," he said.

"What about whether *you* mind?" she asked.

"You do what you think you should," he said, in that forthright north-country voice. "If any of the lads at work make any cracks I'll smack their heads together."

Gloria gave a funny little laugh. Her husband said hoarsely, "Goodbye, lass," and rang off. Gloria put the receiver down slowly, and Palfrey saw the tears in her eyes: in those moments a pleasant-faced but ordinary-looking woman became quite beautiful. Soon, out of the tears and the passing beauty came a bubbling little laugh, and words came bubbling, too.

"I don't know what my Dad would have said, or Mum, for that matter." Then she put her hands out to Palfrey. "You will look after my children, won't you?"

"As well as I possibly can," Palfrey promised.

She gripped his hands, looked into his face for a few seconds, and then asked, "Why do I seem to know you, doctor? Where have I seen you before?"

"You've seen my photographs in the newspapers, you've seen me on television at times of crisis, only a few months ago when there was a great scare about women going barren —"

"Oh, *now* I know!" she cried, her eyes lighting up. "And there are some books about you. You're — *Dr. Palfrey!*"

"That's right," Palfrey said.

"My goodness!" exclaimed Gloria Adamson. "It's like mixing with the crowned heads!"

And she looked happy — although her whole body might be impregnated with radio-active dust, and before long she might die.

On the television screens of the nation that night she looked sad, wistful, scared perhaps, but always composed. When the pictures of her bathed in pale light were shown, she looked quite lovely; woman, as idealised by man; the body beautiful.

Stefan Andromovitch watched, so did Joyce Morgan, so did nearly every man and woman and child in Great Britain. Only in a few of the main centres was there any life in the streets, even the heart of London, in Piccadilly, Leicester Square and Soho, seemed deserted. Waiters, chefs and kitchen staff, stood or sat by the empty tables, watching the screen.

In the great houses of the land, people watched.

In the big apartments and the houses of the rich, people dropped everything and watched.

In the slum areas and the crowded places where the workers lived, everyone watched. And across Europe millions joined the watchers as the drama was played out, for it was relayed by Eurovision, while across the Atlantic millions watched as it was relayed by Telstar. In addition to these countless millions, hundreds of millions more listened to the simultaneous radio broadcast. Great crowds gathered in India and Pakistan, in Africa, in Russia and in China, as a commentator translated. The peoples of the whole world knew what was taking place; knew of the green dust and the horror it could mean; knew that all mankind was facing a common danger.

Palfrey, who was commentating on television, linking up the various aspects of the situation, sensed what was happening. Gloria Adamson was transformed from being a simple wife and mother, into the hope of the world, representing the hopes not only of women but of man. The curious thing was that although most of the pictures had been taken when she was not aware of the significance of what she was doing, she was touched with some quality which carried into the homes and the hearts and the hopes of people.

And Palfrey explained what had happened and how they, the authorities, had selected Gloria as the focal point of the investigation, now and again he explained in non-clinical language the nature of the tests. And he kept saying one thing in many different ways.

"*If Mrs. Adamson is proved to be free of any effects of*

radio-activity, then we can be reasonably sure that we all are . . .

"We are of course carrying out hundreds of similar tests, we shall not be guided simply by this one . . ."

There would be shots of nuclear research stations, of laboratories where radio-active dust was harnessed and used to create nuclear energy, of scientists at work — as Philip Carr had worked so often, handling the deadly substance through thick windows, wearing every kind of protection needed; and there were other pictures, showing the great green clouds in the sky, showing the dust drifting downwards until it covered the fields and the rooftops and the streets and the people.

"We have to face the fact that if this dust, which is lying thick over a huge swathe cut through the agricultural and industrial heart of England, is radio-active then we the people, everyone touched by the dust, is in grave danger. The ultimate situation could be worse even than that in Hiroshima, when the first atomic blast was so decisive in the war in the Far East. At the moment, no tests show that it is except in very occasional places near the source of the explosion. We cannot be absolutely sure that the radio-activity will not spread; that there is no latent radio-active dust in the green."

There would be pictures of men in protective clothing collecting small quantities of the green dust, of it being conveyed to research laboratories, of the use of the geiger counters.

"This particular sample, taken over a month ago from dust inside a nuclear reactor station in the north of England, is radio-active . . ."

There were the slow, deliberate movements of a research worker moving a geiger counter over the samples, and the suddenly crackling sound, and it was as if the whole world held its breath, and did not breathe until the same man moved the same instrument over some of the green dust. There was a faint, very faint rattle of sound, and the people of the world seemed to gasp for breath.

"The strength of the radio-activity in this sample is very

low, almost negligible," Palfrey said, *"but we cannot be sure there are not stronger concentrations. Here, for instance, is the same test being carried out on dust which was taken from the main site of the explosion. You will see that it is less green . . ."*

The geiger counter's crackle was much louder, and fear came back into the hearts and the minds of men. As if to hold it in check, the picture switched to Gloria again; to doctors taking blood from the vein in the bend of her left arm . . . of a tiny piece of skin being removed from the back of her hand, under a local anaesthetic . . . of saliva being taken by a plastic tongue depressor, of mucus from a nostril.

"If any of these samples reveal the presence of radio-activity in any form then we will have to accept the fact that all who were exposed to the suspected contamination are affected . . . If there are no indications then we have every reason to believe that everyone is clean . . . I have information which tells that seventy other people, undergoing the same tests as these on Mrs. Adamson, are yielding the same results."

Pictures flashed on and off the screen, of other people undergoing various tests. Yet more showed the faces of the doctors and scientists involved, of the eagerness, indeed the hope that showed in faces which had been set in anxiety when the tests began. There was a change, too, in Palfrey's expression as some reports were brought into the studio from which he was broadcasting. He read five, silently, and then he looked straight out at the millions of people who were watching and said:

"I will read this report, which is typical of all that have just come in . . . There are no traces of radio-activity contamination on any of the people selected for test . . . There is none on Mrs. Adamson or her children. And all the authorities concerned declare that if the contamination existed the tests carried out would be positive by now."

All over the world there was a great relief in the tension; all over the world people began to move from their seats, to look at each other and even to talk. And Palfrey appeared to be smiling with a relief which touched everyone in the studio. Then suddenly his expression changed and his voice grew sharper and he went on with great precision:

"The dust was radio-active at the scene of the explosion. It now appears that it spread as far as an invisible cloud of some other dust, or some form of wave induced by men whose identity is not yet known. This other dust, or wave, cleansed the atmosphere and in so doing turned the dust green. These unknown men have now demonstrated their power to control radio-activity; earlier, they demonstrated their ability to control sound. They have made discoveries which can be of inestimable value to mankind, such knowledge should belong not to a group of individuals but its advantages should be made available throughout the world.

"What we have seen is a demonstration of great power.

"What we now need from these men is a demonstration of goodwill, the sharing of that power with all mankind."

13

The Power

THE PICTURE ON the screens faded; Palfrey's voice faded, too. Yet everywhere in the world those last words echoed, and carved themselves deeply in the minds of men. The intellectuals and the sophisticated understood and retained what he had said word by word. Those who at one time would have scoffed at his call for 'goodwill to all mankind', the cynics and the sages, did not scoff, for they had been as fearful as anyone during the telecast; had been able to project their minds to the horror that had threatened. Moreover, they caught the implications in the words and in the tone of Palfrey's voice: that had the insulation by wave or chemical not been thrown around the site of the explosion then the horror would have become real.

And it could still become real. In some places, it was.

For already inside the area of The Project men and women and cattle were dying, and others were very sick. Great blood spots appeared beneath the skin, an hour aged some victims by years. Great sickness fell upon them all, dreadful fevers, awful vomiting, loss of all vigour, even of the strength to move.

Yet only a few yards from some who suffered so, others were untouched; that protective wall, or wave, had worked a miracle.

The intellectuals, then, understood this; and understood that Palfrey had declared his own helplessness, at least for the time being. As fervently as he, they wanted the demonstration of goodwill.

The ordinary people understood the need with equal depth of feeling. Many had a sense of doom, but most of great relief. They had come over the years to trust Palfrey in time of great danger and his presence on the screen had given them even greater reason to trust him. Among the people of simplicity, the meek, the naive, there was deep trust in some power behind Palfrey. Some called this God, and others goodness and others could hardly define their feeling but only that there existed a protective arm, and that in some strange way Palfrey could call upon it for protection.

Palfrey himself felt a strange mixture of relief and tension.

He went with Gloria to a rendezvous already arranged with her husband, between Coventry and Nuneaton, in a farmhouse taken over by Z5. He was not surprised to find James Adamson a solid, stocky man with a jutting chin and very bright, direct eyes.

"So it wasn't a waste of time," he said to Palfrey.

"Nothing has ever been more valuable," Palfrey said.

"You won't want Glory again, will you?"

"I don't expect to," Palfrey said, "except for daily check-ups for a while." He smiled faintly. "There will be no more demonstrations."

Adamson chuckled, tucked his wife's arm beneath his, and turned towards the waiting car. Palfrey went back into the farmhouse, where he was in direct radio contact with Z5's London headquarters. He called Joyce, and Stefan answered for her.

"She's sleeping, Sap," he said. "I discovered that she hadn't slept for nearly twenty-four hours. Do you need her urgently?"

"Let her sleep," Palfrey said. "What has the general reaction been?"

"Uniformly good," Stefan told him, and added with a chuckle in his voice, "Even the Kremlin sent a message of congratulation. But —"

"They want to know more about the power of The Project and if there is one in Russia," Palfrey interrupted.

"You cannot imagine how desperately they want information," answered Stefan. "They want to know how great the power is. They cannot quite conceive that any individual or any group of individuals possess as much power as these men seem to have." When Palfrey didn't answer, he went on, "I will study each report from overseas as it comes in, and have a précis ready for you when you get back. Do you yet know when I can expect you?"

"No," Palfrey said. "But within two hours, I hope. Stefan —"

"Yes?"

"Has there been any word at all from The Project?"

Even as he uttered the words he knew the folly of them. Had there been the slightest hint of a message from the leaders of The Project, it would have been the first thing Stefan would have told him. He was asking for the moon, betraying his desperate need to meet and discuss the situation with the V.I.P.s who had given such an overwhelming demonstration of their power.

"None," Stefan said, simply.

"Is Philip there?"

"Yes."

"What is his reaction?"

"Admiration for you and fear for his Janey."

"Ah," Palfrey said. "Fear for her."

"He thinks that she must have died in the explosion," said Stefan. "That only the most important people in The Project would have been taken to safety and he doesn't see any reason why she should be considered of such importance. But he has rested, Sap, and is anxious to know what he can do." When Palfrey didn't reply, Stefan went on, "The vital need is to contact the leaders of The Project."

"Yes," Palfrey said. "Yes. And the only hope seems to be finding out where they are. If they were so anxious not to have their secrets discovered that they destroyed the whole plant, and most of the brilliant men in it, we can be absolutely sure the research has been duplicated elsewhere. There *are* other plants and other research workers."

"Yes," Stefan agreed. "It was always likely that there was more than one Project — unlikely that such experiments and research would depend on the security of one plant. And it was always probable that we were dealing with evil men. It did not take the cold-blooded murder of all who were at The Project here to tell us how ruthless they are."

"The question is, how much power do they have," Palfrey said, heavily.

An hour later, he started out for London.

That was the time when Gloria was looking into her husband's craggy face, feeling the warmth and weight of his arms. He was asleep, for half-an-hour and more he had been on the point of dropping off. The children were asleep in the room they shared, the excitements of the day forgotten.

It was the time when the cordon of soldiers, police and civil defence workers reached the area of destruction; on one side of an invisible wall, there was no evidence of atomic radiation. On the other side the radiation was concentrated sometimes to over 1,000 rontgens. Experts from all over the world arrived at a base camp in a village which had escaped total destruction, but which had been evacuated.

And it was the time when most of the people of England slept . . . The time when Philip Carr went over his written report time and time again . . . When messages began to come into the Operations Room of Z5 from different agents, with reports of the arrival of jet planes with vertical take-off and landing. One landed without permission at Boston airport and twelve passengers and crew, and took off at once in a privately-owned conventional aircraft, also without control tower authority. All attempts to trace it by radar or reconnaissance aircraft failed. The report said,

"Immediately after take-off, much sooner than usual, all sight and sound of the aircraft disappeared."

There was a similar report from Cape Town, South Africa; a third in Perth, Western Australia, one from New Delhi, another from Buenos Aires. In every case, landing was so fast and the transfer to the other aircraft so quickly done that the authorities could not even delay them.

A report came from Siberia . . .

Stefan was studying this as Palfrey was being driven through the streets of the West End of London, towards the Elite Hotel, in Piccadilly. Behind the new luxury hotel were the narrow streets, and the old and new buildings of London; across Piccadilly itself was Green Park, and beyond, Buckingham Palace and St. James's Park. His car pulled up outside the main entrance, in a side street off Piccadilly, and his Jamaican driver jumped out and opened the door.

"Are you all right, Dr. Palfrey?"

"Fine, Miki, thanks."

"Do you know we've been followed?" The Jamaican's face seemed very shiny in the street lamp, his eyes were bright, but his voice was low-pitched and he hardly moved his lips.

"And I think whoever is following me has been followed too," Palfrey replied.

"That's one sure thing," said the Jamaican, his teeth flashing. "You know what you're doing, sir!"

Palfrey smiled, and turned towards the hotel, and wondered. He had known that he might be followed, of course, and also that Z5 agents had tailed the following car. There was some comfort in the knowledge that Project workers were now watching him closely; it suggested that they might want to talk to him. He had uttered those last words on television in a near-desperate appeal: "*Let us talk.*" But there was not yet the slightest hint of response, unless it was that the cue had been followed.

He went into the brightly lit foyer of the hotel. Pale-faced night porters stood about; a well-dressed man was dozing in an easy chair. The bar was still open but he saw only one man sitting at it. He walked to the elevators and stepped into one which took him to the second floor, stepped out, and entered another, opposite, which took him downwards. The general means of access to the headquarters of Z5 varied frequently, so that no-one who discovered the entrance during one period could get access to it during another. He had not been followed into the hotel, but any of the porters or the man drowsing or the man at the bar might be an agent of The Project.

The lift stopped at the first of three floors built deep into the earth. This was the main staff and offices floor, with some sleeping accommodation; the one below was the main Operations Floor, which had his own office and his apartment, as well as Joyce Morgan's; and it was where Stefan would stay. Below were the laboratories. Some detention cells, waiting rooms: here the organisation had to use pressure-force, even torture to win vital information. There were times when he would lie sleepless for hours debating the moral issues involved; but always he concluded that these hateful methods were necessary at times of extreme danger. What a sickening world it was!

He went along to the main offices, as busy by night as by day; all the lamps here gave off a kind of imitation daylight. Howard, the man in charge of the Department was the Information and Records Officer, with a system of keeping records of agents, of suspects — men or women believed to be hostile to Z5 or the world at large. Howard was a short but broad-shouldered man with a large head, nearly bald, except at the sides where his hair was nut brown. Palfrey had warned him he was coming, and Howard was in his private office which led off a huge room stacked with filing cabinets in which documents as well as tapes were stored.

"Hallo, Sap. That was quite a job you did tonight." Howard had a lively smile.

"Thanks. What kind of a job have you done?" countered Palfrey.

"I haven't had any luck at all," Howard answered. "We

haven't a single line on any agent of The Project except the prisoners we took yesterday, I mean." The smile only half-flashed. "And —" he paused.

"Go on."

"We thought we had tabs on several after they started the search for Philip Carr, and they've vanished. Simply gone. What we had was little enough but it was pure gold compared with what we have now."

Palfrey said, "Keep trying."

Next, he went down to the third floor: the floor he disliked almost to a point of hatred. The man in charge here had the ironic name of Merribell, and he had been in charge only for six months. Also warned of Palfrey's coming, he was in the same kind of office as Howard, but beyond the office were small laboratories and small cells — cells which had been soundproofed. The men who had been captured after they had waited for Philip Carr were here. Palfrey did not need to ask what processes had been used on them, what agony each man had suffered. This was the aspect of his job which so often kept him sleepless at night.

Merribell was one of the most cold-blooded men he had ever known. He was no sadist, but had no compunction at all about causing pain and terror if it was the only way to get vital information. In his youth he had suffered his own agonies in a Chinese prison, suspected of spying, and to this day he bore the scars, on his back and in his mind. He had one other proven quality: absolute belief in the political freedom of man and full acceptance of the rights of men, whatever their race or wealth or creed or colour, to that freedom. To look at, he was a rather dull person with little expression in his small, deep-set and hooded eyes. He had a snub nose with wide nostrils and thin lips above a rounded chin. He looked weak rather than cruel.

"Good evening, Dr. Palfrey."

"Good evening, Professor."

"I am afraid I have bad news for you," Merribell stated.

"None of them has talked?"

"Oh, they have talked," the other answered. "But they know nothing. Whenever they have driven or piloted these V.I.P.s they have simply carried them to certain air-fields or ports, and returned. They have no knowledge of the destination of their masters. If you have doubts —" he led the way to one of the cells, the door of which had a one-way window. Palfrey tightened his lips as he looked in.

One man was inside.

He was huddled on a small bed, in a state of absolute exhaustion, and when Merribell pressed a bell push he began to shiver and shrink close to the wall, his face working and his lips trembling. Saliva frothed at his lips. Palfrey nodded and turned away.

"I have records of their statements —"

"Let me see transcriptions, please," Palfrey interrupted. He read these in the office and had no doubt at all that the prisoners had been driven to the absolute limits of their endurance. Merribell watched him with obvious satisfaction, and as he finished said,

"I do assure you there is no point in trying again."

"I'm quite sure there isn't," Palfrey said.

Now he went to the second, or main operational floor, and walked along first to the Operations Room. Stefan and Philip were talking to one of the operators, who sat in front of a section of the big control panel, taking messages from European agents. There was something close to excitement in Stefan's eyes as he spun round.

"Sap — I think we have traced one!"

"Where?" Palfrey asked, sharply.

"In the Urals," Stefan answered.

"*Russia!*"

"Yes, indeed, Russia."

"Have you told the Kremlin?"

"Not yet," Stefan answered. "I want first to be sure, and also to discuss the situation with you." Palfrey's hand was tight and almost painful on Stefan's shoulder. "We have an agent at a workers' camp near Belusha in the foothills of the

Urals, and he was on duty when the aircraft virtually fell out of the skies and disappeared into a valley. Two other guards saw it but assumed that this was an experimental aircraft — there are many such. Zuka, our man, is quite sure that the aircraft fitted the description we sent out. He can pick up our wavelength without difficulty, and was able to call us back only ten minutes ago."

"If it is true, that's our first break," Palfrey said, his excitement as great as Stefan's. "The quicker we're there —"

There was a moment of silence before Philip Carr raised his hands and dropped them heavily to his sides, looked for a moment very directly at Stefan, and then as directly at Palfrey.

"With all respect to Stefan," he said, "can we trust Moscow? Doesn't it strike you as peculiar that there's no trace of any of the others but there is of this one. Are you absolutely sure this isn't a trick, Sap? That this whole thing isn't Soviet inspired?"

14

Doubting Philip

PHILIP'S WORDS CAME out slowly and deliberately; there was nothing spontaneous about them, obviously they were deeply considered. There was something in his sharp-cut face which held stubbornness, as if he knew that no-one who heard him would disagree but he wasn't going to shift easily from this position. To Palfrey, the shock was greater because he had never before heard an agent express such doubts. Every man who joined was thoroughly screened; every man had a history of belief in a world authority; of belief that in some issues the world — and so Z5 — must come before one's own country. It was so much part of the creed of Z5 that it was hard to believe that a man such as Stefan, the deputy leader, could be doubted. But this was doubt, cast quite deliberately, on his loyalty and integrity. The agent at the controls was listening to a message coming through on the high-frequency radio, but he looked at Philip as if shocked.

"Philip," Stefan said, in his mild voice with its precise English, "if all the planes but one had disappeared and the one had been traced to the United States, say, or to France, would you express the same doubts?"

Quietly, Philip answered, "Not unless you were an American or a Frenchman."

"And what makes you so question my integrity?"

"I think all of us have a soft spot for our own country," Philip replied. "And Russians have a softer spot than most.

As we're talking about this, perhaps I should finish. I simply can't believe that a Russian who lives most of the time in Moscow under the shadow of the Kremlin, the Politbureau and the Presidium, can ever put world interests above his country's."

"You mean you think I am a spy working for Russia within Z5?" asked Stefan.

"I think you may be," said Philip. "I think you probably are."

Palfrey felt a burning sense of anger as he heard Philip, so young in Z5's service, talking to the man who had been in from the beginning, who had proved himself time and time again. It would be easy to rasp angrily at Philip, to take away his privileges, to say that such doubts cancelled out all his qualification for being an agent of Z5. Then Palfrey saw a frown of bewilderment pass over the doubter's face, glanced up at Stefan, and saw that he was smiling. There was something so radiant in his expression that it was almost the face of a giant cherub, truly and highly amused.

"So," he said. "You have much to learn, Philip!"

"Philip —" began Palfrey.

"Let me finish," pleaded Stefan, and his smile at Palfrey was just as radiant. "Philip thinks as millions think — scratch a Russian and you find a militant Communist who will live, work and die for his cause. Well, loyalty as an abstract quality is as commendable in a Russian Communist or a fascist or a democrat. And I love Russia — Philip is quite right, each of us has a special soft spot for our own country. Haven't you for England, Sap?"

"Of course."

"What Philip hasn't had is a long time in the Organisation to see how it gets hold of a man," went on Stefan. "When do you want to start for Moscow?"

"As soon as we can," Palfrey said.

"Should we? All of us are near exhaustion point, you in particular need sleep. If we start in six hours, say, we shall gain more in our own vigour than we shall lose in time.

But —" he smiled down at Philip — "Philip has rested. Philip has time to read through the official histories of our various cases, and when he has read of my conflicts with the Soviets, and their doubts of me, I think he will be able to understand and accept me more freely. Will you study the histories, Philip?"

Carr hesitated. His lips began to curve into a smile; he raised his hands in another resigned or helpless gesture, and said:

"Yes. I should have known the establishment would win."

"This establishment has to win," rejoined Stefan. "The world loss would be too heavy if it didn't."

As he finished a green light glowed and a moment later a voice sounded clearly. All three men stood absorbed as they listened.

"The aircraft which was traced to Washington and seen to have some damage on one wing has now been observed flying over Alaska, and is heading for Russia . . . The aircraft which was traced to Cape Town, South Africa, was seen by patrolling aircraft to be struck by lightning and fell into the Indian Ocean off Madagascar . . . Two of the aircraft which flew to Australia were forced down by storm conditions and Australian fighter aircraft caught their pilots. The pilots state that fourteen of the aircraft which left England had instructions to act as decoys and if they could not reach a place named Belusha in the Urals they should destroy themselves . . . Three more of the aircraft are now known to have reached the Urals and vanished near there."

In the space of ten minutes Palfrey and the others learned what it was most vital to learn: that the centre of activity had undoubtedly shifted to Russia.

Palfrey's apartment at Z5 Headquarters could simulate broad daylight, or night's darkness, winter or summer skies, autumn or spring's. When he pulled the blinds in his office-cum-living-room or his bedroom, he looked out on whatever season it was above, even though he was two hundred feet below ground, surrounded by the wet gravel on which most of London was built. Now, as he came out of a modern bathroom buttoning up his pyjama jacket, he went to the window and looked out on starlit bushes and the sky so full of stars. There were a few clouds, drifting very sluggishly.

He went to bed.

On the bedside table was a glass of milk and a tablet; he swallowed the one and washed it down with the other. One *had* to sleep. The stresses of the task itself were too great to try to manage without, and the tablet would not only give him natural sleep but he would have no kind of hangover in the morning. He slid into bed, and drew a sheet and a light-weight blanket over him; the air-conditioning kept the temperature in this room to sixty-nine. For a few moments he browsed, partly over Gloria Adamson, partly over Philip Carr's accusation against Stefan and Stefan's reaction; but mostly about the fact that several of the vertical take-off jets had landed in Russia. It did not occur to him for a moment that Z5 was being wilfully misled, but it was possible that there had been a mistake.

It was equally possible that Russia — not Stefan, not any Z5 agent, but Russia — would attempt to turn the situation to its own advantage. For by now Russia, in fact all the powers great and small, would begin to comprehend the almost unimaginable power now vested in the leaders of The Project.

They could insulate themselves, or anyone, or any place against radio-active air.

They could create silence by insulating themselves and some if not all machines against noise. Either weapon could give to the side which owned it near mastery if not absolute mastery in time of war. Any power would lust for the secret. With it, Russia or China could deride and challenge any other country in the world. So in one way there was a form of validity in Philip's suspicion of Russia.

How should he, Palfrey, respond?

Before he dropped off to sleep, he knew; in fact he had

never had any serious doubt. He must negotiate with Russia as if he could rely absolutely on the Kremlin's attitude towards Z5.

At last, he went to sleep.

And Stefan slept, much more lightly.

Philip read four of the reports, each of one about a case in which Stefan Andromovitch had had to choose between loyalty to his country and loyalty to Z5; unarguably, he had always chosen Z5. Twice, this had led him to disaster, trial and nearly to execution by Russia, but the Presidium had always come round to honouring its pledge to Z5.

"It looks good," Philip said aloud. "There could be a catch in it, but it looks good." He dozed in turn, and was actually asleep, dreaming of Janey, when he was called by an elderly woman, one of Z5's earliest agents who still preferred to serve the organisation.

"Dr. Palfrey is leaving in half-an-hour," she reported. "He would like to see you in his office before he goes." She put a tea tray by his side, and went out. Philip sat up, yawning, but almost at once a picture of Janey passed in front of his mind's eye, and tension replaced the slothfulness. He had shaved and had some toast and marmalade by the time he reached Palfrey's office. Joyce Morgan was there, freshly made-up, youthful-looking and attractive, she reminded him vividly of Janey. Palfrey was sitting in an easy chair, toast and marmalade and coffee on a tray beside him.

"Well," he said. "Are you convinced of Stefan's integrity?"

Philip quietened any reservations he had, and answered, "Yes."

"Good! He's gone ahead of me to Moscow, but I am to catch a plane one hour from now. We are going to ask the Russian authorities to do what the British did: throw a cordon around the Belusha Valley where it seems there may be a Project plant, and make sure no-one can go in and out. Warned by our experience they will have high altitude bombers and fighter-flights to atttack any vertical take-off aircraft which might attempt to escape. Is that all clear?"

"Yes," Philip answered.

"Good," Palfrey said again, and sipped coffee while looking at the other man intently. "There is one thing we lack."

"What's that?" asked Philip.

"Anyone who can identify such leaders as Ashley and Parsons and Ramon. If we find The Project in the valley but those three aren't there, then we can be pretty sure they're hiding out at yet another Project plant."

Philip caught his breath.

"*I* can recognise them," he said.

"That's why I want you with me." Palfrey went on. "Stefan and I want to go to the valley and try to get inside the plant. Will you come with us?" When Philip didn't answer, he continued drily, "Of course, we may all be blasted off the face of the earth. Or we might be taken prisoners. We might be tortured. But I am quite sure that we must find a way of talking to leaders of The Project, and I can see no other possible way."

Quietly, Philip answered, "Yes, I'll come." He gave a snort of a laugh and went on, "If it were only to find out what happened to Janey, I would come."

"I shall be ready in ten minutes," Palfrey said. "I'll meet you at the main lift. Clothes and a case can be sent on."

"I'm always packed," Philip assured him.

Palfrey nodded, and Philip turned and went out. There was a positiveness about his manner, an aggressive kind of 'take me as I am'. Joyce waited until the door had closed on him, then crossed to Palfrey's chair and sat on the arm. Suddenly, they seemed different people, not simply high officials in Z5, but man and woman. And Joyce, here and there a streak of grey in her dark hair, tiny crows' feet at her eyes and lines at her full lips, seemed almost to relax, as if this were their time together.

For years she had been deeply in love with him. Now the love had turned into affection, and she was in love with her husband; but at this moment they were very close.

He was, as he had been for many years, in love with the dream of his dead wife, fond as always of Joyce, touched by her devotion. He had often been tempted to share much more of his life with her than he did: tempted to live with her. There were moments of stress and strain when he marvelled that he had not. There had been other women, and brief *affaires*, but there was never, with him, any pretence of love.

Now, perhaps, they were more like brother and sister.

"Sap," she said earnestly, "be more careful than you've ever been in your life."

"As careful as I can be," he promised.

"Do you think you should take Carr?"

"Yes."

"Why?"

"To watch him closely."

"Why?"

"A man in love can do unpredictable things," Palfrey said. "In any case he's the only one we have who's seen any of these V.I.P.s." He put a hand on her wrist and shifted his position. "I must get a move on."

She stood up, so that he could move, but she kept a firm hold on his arm.

"Sap?"

"You can worry too much, you know," Palfrey said.

"Yes. But — you haven't really told me about The Project, what you think, what you feel that you should do."

"There hasn't been much time," Palfrey observed ruefully. "And there still isn't time to tell you all I'd like to. As for what I think — I really don't know that I've any clearly defined opinions. Did you hear the tapes of the talks I had with Philip when I first saw him in Chelsea?"

"Yes," Joyce answered. "Among the things he said was that people could do good in their own way, that they have made great discoveries of enormous value to mankind."

"In short, the ends could justify the means. Is that what he was implying?"

"Yes," Joyce repeated. "And they've killed and tortured to get their own way."

"They are not the only ones," Palfrey said, taking her hands. After what seemed a long time he went on, "Did you go down to the lower floor today to watch Merribell work on the prisoners from Euston? The torture methods we use? Have you seen the prisoners since? Have you paused to think what we do for what we believe is right?"

After a long pause, Joyce asked, as if astounded.

"Sap, what's got into you?"

"I don't know," answered Palfrey, gruffly. "Philip Carr, perhaps. And the facts. If these people can insulate us against radio-activity, if it can be safely used so that we can have nuclear power for safe usage — Joyce," he broke off. "Joyce. If there's a way to find out, then I have to try."

"Of course you have," she said gently.

He drew her forward and touched her forehead with his lips — and then quite suddenly and without a moment's warning even to himself, he slid his arm round her, kissed her full on the lips, and held her very close.

When he drew back, her eyes reminded him of Stefan's in their radiance.

Stefan Andromovitch stepped out of the British military plane at Moscow Airport, was correctly received by two officers of the Red Army and one civilian whom he knew: Igor Novosky, the liaison officer between the Soviet government and Z5. A large car which resembled a twenty-year-old American Packard was drawn up near the aircraft, and as they walked towards this, Novosky asked:

"Where is Dr. Palfrey?"

"He will be on the next flight."

"Why did he not come with you?"

"To lessen any risk of us both dying together."

"Do you seriously fear attack?"

"Comrade," Stefan said in his gentlest voice. "I do not fear, but I am always very cautious."

"I understand," said Novosky, stiffly.

Stefan sat in the back of the car, and looked about the wide streets, recognising the tall buildings in the distance, the mammoth university and the fine new apartment buildings which were no longer just shells hiding the slums behind, but stood proudly row after row, as if to challenge the far off Western world. It was a long time before they reached the great squares, and a crescent moon shone with Mogul splendour on the onion-turreted spires of St. Basil's Cathedral, on the high walls of the Kremlin, on GUM, the palatial department store which stood in Victorian magnificence opposite the tomb which held the remains of Lenin. The car rumbled across the cobbles where marching feet and armoured tanks and death-dealing rockets so often thundered.

This morning there was quiet — peacefulness.

The gates leading into the Kremlin were opened and as the car went through, were closed again by silent guards. A pale moon shone and the stars were dusted as with a mist in the skies; the mist of dawn. The buildings inside the Kremlin walls were in stark outline, mostly dark. Here and there a yellow square of light showed, and street lamps glowed. Stefan, who knew exactly where they were going, sat with his knees pressing against the back of the seat in front, uncomfortable as he always was in cars and chairs made for men of ordinary size.

They passed the great bell, with the huge gap where it had broken when dropped when being delivered to the palace where it was to ring. The bell of peace which had never tolled carried such irony. They swept along past the huddle of churches with their gold onion tops making them look like minarets. They passed the great armoury, now a proud museum of Russia's past, where even the Tsars were acknowledged. Soon they were within sight of the wall which separated the Kremlin from the Muscva River and, from a high spot, could see the pale surface of the river, wide and calm, as it reflected the growing light of day.

15

The Cunning Saint

THE CAR TURNED towards a building which was squat and modern, passed through another pair of gates which opened barely wide enough to allow them through and closed so quickly that the rear of the car seemed in danger; but there were inches to spare. Two soldiers, carrying rifles, stood at the foot of a flight of stone steps, and two others by a door at the top. The man with Stefan showed his credentials and the door opened. Stefan got out and stretched himself like a great bear. No one spoke as they went up the steps, and through the open doorway. Beyond were bright lights, two or three little groups of people all eyeing the newcomers intently, but neither Stefan nor his guides — or were they guards? — spoke until they reached a room with iron-studded doors. This was also a relic from a castle long-since burned down; beautiful, in an ogreish way. A man in uniform examined their passes, including Stefan's, then announced them through a microphone built into the wall by the door.

"They may enter," a man responded, and at once the doors opened and they went into a room with panelled walls, a round table, with chairs all about it, a man sitting in a larger chair than the others, with a painting of Lenin on the wall above his head. There were other paintings — of Kruschev, Voroshilov, even Stalin; of the present Soviet leaders and, opposite the one of Lenin, the heroes of the Soviet Union, including the first astronauts.

The man in the chair was startling to look at; his head and face were clean-shaven, there appeared to be no hair at all. He was dressed in a lounge suit with a high, almost 'mod' collar, which made the smooth hairlessness of his face look even stranger. There was nothing remarkable about his features which were rounded, almost childlike; but his eyes, dark blue, had nothing remotely childlike about them.

This was Boris Shakalov, the leader of Soviet espionage in countries of the outside world; a man, who, when he had been in charge of counter-espionage within the U.S.S.R., had caused as much fear and trembling as the age-long-dreaded, long-dead Beria.

He waved to chairs; and as they sat, Stefan stretching his long legs under the table, a man wheeled in a trolley with tea, coffee, biscuits and sweetmeats. Shakalov spoke as if the man were not there.

"Good-morning, Comrade Andromovitch."

"Good-morning, Comrade Shakalov."

"I expected Dr. Palfrey to be with you."

"He will arrive in an aircraft which left England an hour later than mine."

"Was that a safety precaution?"

"Yes."

"Why did you think it necessary?"

Shakalov spoke in a clear, pleasant voice, barely opening his mouth, so that the words seemed to escape, rather than be deliberately uttered.

"There is a risk that we will be attacked by agents of The Project."

"You were not followed once you flew over the East German border," Shakalov stated. "Could not your friends in Britain and in Nato protect you, also."

"We do not know for certain what the protection must be against," Stefan retorted. "In any case, both Dr. Palfrey and I carry a great deal of information in our heads; it is surely better to try to be certain that whatever the danger, one of us survives."

"I will not dispute that," Shakalov conceded. He sipped coffee and broke one of the flat biscuits in his fingers. "I hope Dr. Palfrey's lateness will not delay a report."

"It will not, Comrade. In fact between you and me there will be no need for translation, so time will be saved." As he paused, something that might have been a smile touched Shakalov's lips. "Have you traced the arrival of the vertical take-off jet aircraft?"

"Yes," Shakalov answered, and the smile hovered.

"Was it near the valley above Belusha?"

"More precisely, at Hansa."

"Has the cordon been thrown about the valley?"

"It has," stated Shakalov, and went on as if with a quirk of humour. "Everything your man Zuka said has been proved correct. One day, Comrade, I shall be interested to know how you persuaded Zuka to serve you instead of the Soviet."

Stefan sipped coffee, as he responded, "He who serves the Organisation serves the world. He who serves the world serves the Soviet."

"That is a very novel philosophy of loyalty," retorted Shakalov drily. "We must discuss it."

"Is Zuka still at his post, Comrade?"

"Yes, and will remain there."

"Did the others with him report the arrival of the jet?"

"No."

"You might assume from this, that Zuka served the Soviet better than those who saw nothing," said Stefan, tartly.

"I take your point, Comrade."

"Has the valley been kept under close observation?"

"Very close indeed," answered Shakalov.

"Are there indications of where the aircraft landed?"

"Yes." Shakalov pressed a button close to his right hand. There was a faint whirring noise, and then a screen appeared in place of one of the panels and the beam from a projector shone on to it. All of the men present could see simply by turning their heads. A picture appeared very out of focus, was put into focus and showed a stretch of countryside, sparsely dotted with trees, and grass or scrub showing everywhere. "If you follow the line of the trees," went on the espionage leader, "you will see a faint but positive outline of a square which covers some fifty feet by fifty. Do you perceive?"

At first, Stefan could not see it, but as he watched the outline appeared, and as he said: "Yes!" with excitement sharp in his voice, a little arrow appeared on the screen tracing the square. Quickly, the arrow moved and traced a second square. It moved again, and Shakalov talked over its jerky movements.

"There are six such outlines, Comrade, and according to your reports from England there were six which opened, with three aircraft taking off from each. Is that right?"

"Yes."

"Four arrived here, so there are fourteen others."

"Yes."

"Has any been traced?"

"Yes," Stefan said, and passed on what he knew about all planes heading for Russia, and the pilots' stories of some being decoys.

"Your other agents are as competent as Zuka," the shaven-headed man said with reluctant admiration, and his smile hovered again. "Are you satisfied that these aircraft which have landed on what I have called Project Two, are in the valley?"

"Yes," answered Stefan. "What is more important —" he broke off.

"Whether we can raid the valley without causing them to do what they did in England," Shakalov said quietly.

"You mean, whether they know we are aware of their presence," said Stefan.

"Is there a way of being certain?"

"A possible way," Stefan answered.

"Explain, please," urged Shakalov.

Stefan Andromovitch hesitated.

A great deal was spinning through his mind, mostly questions, with the main question about the man who sat opposite him. He knew Shakalov as well as anyone could; once, he had worked for him, and for many years he had worked for Z5 at the same time. And he knew that in dealing with Shakalov it was necessary to begin aggressively, not to allow him to take the initiative. But it was possible to push too far; he could be as adamant as the Berlin Wall, as immovable as a mountain. The problem was to judge when to ease the pressure and allow him to take the initiative, or at least, defer to him. Shakalov beckoned the man with the trolley for more coffee, then motioned to Stefan; and a gesture of outward courtesy could indicate a toughening of resistance. So could the further relaxing of the other's lips into a smile.

"Or perhaps you prefer to wait for your leader Palfrey to explain," he said, taunting.

"Comrade," said Stefan, leaning forward earnestly. "You know that I am the deputy leader of Z5, that Dr. Palfrey and I have been friends and associates for over twenty years, and —" he spread his large, beautifully shaped hands over the table, palms downwards; and his smile was broader than Shakalov's, his eyes wide with innocence and simplicity — "you also know my allegiance to Z5."

"I do, indeed, Comrade." There was something near a threat in Shakalov's voice.

"So —" Stefan spread his fingers, as if drawing attention to the shape of the nails and the silky hairs on the backs of them and the backs of his hands and wrists, "you will understand my diffidence when saying that he remains an Englishman and I a Russian and there are gaps in our understanding."

"Yes," replied Shakalov, "this I can believe."

"This Andromovitch is a shrewd one," the Russian said to himself. "He has the face of a saint and the mind of a Machiavelli. He must have, or he would not have been able to serve two masters for so long. Now he has decided that

*he needs my help. It will be fascinating to find out in what
way.*"

"Dr. Palfrey," Stefan said, "has rare courage."

"A great many men have courage," retorted Shakalov.
"Both friends and enemies. In what way does Dr. Palfrey
express his courage over this affair?"

"He is persuaded that among the leaders of The Project
there may be men who could be turned to the benefit of
mankind," said Andromovitch.

"They all appear more likely to be enemies of society,"
retorted Shakalov, roughly. "Is it courage or folly to hold
such an opinion?"

"It is courage to wish to visit them and find out what he
can of their motives."

Shakalov sat upright, so sharply that it was clear that he
was impressed.

"To visit them at their plant in Hansa?"

"Yes," answered Stefan.

"*Alone?*"

"No, Comrade — with me and also with the one agent of
Z5 who has been inside one Project plant and escaped."

"Ahhh," breathed Shakalov. "Philip Carr?"

"You also are well-informed."

"What can Dr. Palfrey seriously hope to achieve by such
a visit?"

"Find out whether there is a way in which we — the world
and every nation in it — can come to terms with The Project
and whatever the leaders are planning." When Shakalov did
not speak, but sat bolt upright, staring as if he were trying
to read Stefan's thoughts, Stefan went on, "If we are allowed
to come away, then there will be the possibility of discussions
on a high level. If we are not —" Stefan shrugged. "Then
obviously The Project will be proved a threat which must
be contained."

He sat back, stretched his legs beneath the table to his
fullest, touched Shakalov's foot, which was quickly with-

drawn. The silence lasted for a long time. Stefan became aware of the breathing of the two men, in Shakalov's service, who had brought him here. The beam of light from the projector faded; the faint whirr of the machine died away, the panel slid back into position.

At last, Shakalov stirred.

"And you wish me to recommend this to the Presidium?"

"Your approval is the only hope of their agreement," Stefan replied.

"I must be very careful," Shakalov warned himself. "If I recommend this and it fails, I will be blamed." He broke off in his thinking, watching Andromovitch, who sat so calmly, so peacefully, his gentle voice inviting him, Shakalov, to take steps towards his own downfall. "First — is it a sensible move? ... Second — will the Presidium accept a proposal from Palfrey? ... Third, if they go and do not return, is the position any worse?"

"Comrade," said Stefan, into the other's reverie.

"Yes, Comrade?"

"Will you permit me to make a suggestion?"

"You have not been backward in making suggestions!"

"The urgency of the matter is so pressing," murmured Stefan apologetically, and he spread his hands again. "If you were to present this proposal as emanating from you, it might well have a greater chance of acceptance than if it were known to come from Dr. Palfrey."

Shakalov's lips turned down, and he paused again.

"Yes," he said to himself, "he is a man of a simplicity which out-reaches the cunning of most men. He proposes that I should take all the credit if it is successful, and the blame if it should fail. But would there be blame? Can anything different be done?" He probed into the possibilities while Stefan Andromovitch sat like a statue by Michelangelo, radiating goodwill, innocence, integrity. He thought,

"Andromovitch doubtless knows that the President is at the other end of a telephone, expecting to hear from me."

"Comrade," Stefan spoke again when he felt sure that the silence had lasted long enough.

Shakalov stirred, as if out of a stupor.

"What is it, Andromovitch?"

"It is a matter of urgency," Stefan reminded him. "If the men in The Project are given ample time to be sure of your surveillance then they may act before you have reached a decision." He shrugged his shoulders, as if with apology. "The urgency is not of my making."

"No," admitted Shakalov, after another, briefer pause. "It is certainly not of your making. If you will excuse me, Comrade." He pushed his chair back, and bowed stiffly from the waist, and as Stefan rose, turned towards the door, turned back almost at once, and then added: "Perhaps you would like to go to meet Dr. Palfrey's aircraft, while this matter is under consideration."

"I would like that very much," Stefan said. "You are very kind, Comrade." He also bowed.

A few minutes later he was led out of the room and when he reached the gate, the sun was already high in the East, shining with savage splendour on the gold of the turrets and the steeples, giving a glory of light and life and colour. As the car turned out of the Kremlin into Red Square, dozens of people were moving about, a crowd of students stood close to Lenin's tomb, while the many-domed cathedral seemed to be aflame. A queue of people was filing towards the big department store which looked like some huge government department building.

The white buildings of the University rose high, clear, imposing; and now the streets about it were crowded with students, young men and women laughing and talking together as they came off the grey buses, and off bicycles, even a few private cars and trucks. As all this fell behind him, Stefan heard the droning of aircraft in the sky.

Suddenly, he saw one catch fire — fire which began with an explosion in one of its two engines. And Stefan was instantly aware of two facts. The aircraft he had come on had had two engines, and the plane which had caught fire had the red, white and blue markings of the British Royal Air Force. The man beside him watched, also, and suddenly urged the driver, "Hurry, hurry."

The students looked upwards, towards the fire in the sky. So did the shoppers.

So did the people.

And as they stared the roar of the aircraft ceased. So did that of other machines, of cars and trucks and buses, of factories and of shops.

Moscow was a city of silence as the burning aircraft swooped towards the ground and the car with Stefan in it hurtled towards the airport as if through a tunnel from which all sound had vanished.

The silence fell upon the Kremlin, also; and hushed the voice of Boris Shakalov as he stood before the Committee of Three which made whatever swift decisions had to be made in the name of the whole nation.

16

The Decision

PALFREY SAT BACK in his seat and looked out on Moscow. He had been here a dozen, perhaps twenty times, and the city of great domes and mammoth buildings, the city where Christian and Muslim seemed to meet together and yet where all were infidels. Moscow had always looked impressive, the area near the Kremlin and Red Square especially so. But he had never come so soon after dawn, never seen it so resplendent. For a few minutes, he forgot even what he had come for; and then he marvelled.

Suddenly, he sensed a difference.

He was aware of silence, and realised on that instant that the noise of the engines had cut out. Yet the plane was flying normally, and he could see the exhaust coming from the engine on his right, nearest him, and the flashes of flame which came all the time.

There was a longer stab of flame than most; then, with awful suddenness, flame engulfed the engine and hid it, and seemed to turn the wing into which it was built into white-hot metal. He gripped the arm of his seat as the co-pliot came from the cabin, a stocky man in uniform, with smoothed-down black hair which reminded Palfrey vaguely of Philip Carr. Carr, who had been up in the cabin, now came back. The aircraft, used for flying senior officers about the world, was more like a civil plane than a military one.

Then, quickly, the sounds came back, including the roaring of the flames, so near the window.

"Spot of trouble, sir," said the co-pilot.

"So I see," said Palfrey. "What's the drill?"

"We're going to try a forced landing."

"The only alternative is to take to the parachutes," remarked Carr. He was smiling, although tight-lipped, and his eyes were very bright. "Any preference, Sap?"

"We're too low for the parachutes," the co-pilot declared. "Fasten your safety-belts — you're already near the emergency exits." He was as calm as if this were simply a drill. And he also flashed a grin. "Tony Griffiths has got out of a lot worse scrapes than this. We should be able to land on one of the strips."

Palfrey nodded as he fastened the belt. Philip, across the aisle, also fastened his.

"Fifty-fifty, I would say."

"Looks about right," agreed Palfrey. He did not feel panic-stricken but was aware of a tightening of muscles at his chest and throat.

Below, the great airfield spread, with its criss-cross of runways; the airport control tower came in sight; so did several ambulances which seemed to be racing in all directions and as many fire-fighting tenders. Palfrey could see all this on either side of the burning engine, the flames from which had settled into long streamers.

He still did not feel actual fear; only that tension.

He knew their chances were much less than fifty-fifty, and he wondered what would happen if he died.

There was Stefan . . .

And there were others who had been trained to take high positions in Z5, but few who knew half — not a quarter — of what he knew. Except Joyce. He saw the possibility that Stefan and Joyce would have to take over, but what would her husband say? He wondered if the leaders of Russia would allow Stefan to go to live in England permanently; whether Philip was nearer right than he, Palfrey, wanted to think.

Philip was peering out of the window, as nearly disinterested as a man could appear.

The aircraft was still on an even keel.

The rumble and bump of the landing gear going down sounded loud.

The airfield itself seemed to disappear and there were only houses, tall buildings, streets dotted with people and with traffic. Then, as they made the inevitable wide turn, the airfield came into sight again, with the rescue vehicles and crews lined up along one runway, and he knew this was going to be the landing run.

Philip flashed another smile.

"Happy landing," he called, and Palfrey actually found himself laughing.

Then the ground seemed to rise up and strike them, there was a bump, a roar, a leap into the air. The aircraft swivelled round, kept on going, then by some miracle slewed back on to the runway. The fire blazed with fierce white heat until suddenly the engine fell off and the plane slewed round again. The driver of an ambulance was goggle-eyed with terror but they missed the vehicle and began to slow down.

The co-pilot came along, holding on to the seats.

"About ready," he announced. "We'll open the exit doors."

One of these opened opposite Palfrey, and he slid to the emergency chute. There was fire everywhere, and stinking smoke, and stinking foam on the runway and the barren ground nearby. The aircraft was almost at a standstill. An ambulance was only twenty yards away, keeping pace. Palfrey steadied himself like a child preparing to slide down a playground chute before he actually began to slide. He went into the squashy foam, banged his head on something soft, rolled over and over, saw the aircraft slide away from him, heard the engines of the rescue craft, deafening, then stopped rolling; and consciousness seemed to ooze out of him.

He was vaguely aware of voices, of men, of being lifted. He was oblivious of time and place. The inside of his head seemed to be full of banging hammers. He was aware of comfort to his body; and then became aware of a voice as precious as it was familiar.

"It's all right, Sap," Stefan was saying. "It's all right."

That was the moment of supreme relief; the moment when Palfrey lost consciousness completely; the moment when Stefan came nearer to despair than he had ever been in his life. He was oblivious of the doctors assuring him that Palfrey *was* all right, and would not die. For Palfrey was needed desperately, now. Not in a few hours' time, not tomorrow, but *now*. And he looked as if he were at death's door, although Philip Carr, who had gone down the chute on the other side, had escaped with hardly a scratch.

Palfrey came round in the emergency hospital at the airfield. Doctors and nurses were examining his left leg and his right hand; and one of them spoke in Russian of which Palfrey had only a smattering. A nurse, glancing at Palfrey, moved towards him, smiling. She had the broad features and the dark eyes of the eastern provinces.

"You do not need to worry," she said in good English. "It is one leg and one hand only which is hurt, and neither of them as badly as it is feared. Your friend, Mr. Andromovitch, will be here soon."

"And the other Englishmen?" Palfrey asked urgently.

"They are well, sir — you do not need to fear."

The tension began to ooze out of Palfrey.

He had some idea of the tremendous effort made to get him mobile; of the way they soothed the pain in his leg and hand; the injections which killed the pain and yet left his mind clear. When Stefan arrived he had an even clearer idea of the big man's anxiety and his relief at finding him as well as he was.

"Because they have agreed, Sap," Stefan announced.

"To letting us approach The Project plant?" Palfrey marvelled.

"Yes. The Presidium has agreed —" Stefan's eyes shone — "to Comrade Shakalov's proposals! There was hope that we could go today but in view of what happened it will be better tomorrow. No," he went on as Palfrey opened his mouth to protest. "Another day is needed to make the military dispositions without allowing The Project guards — and there must be many — to know what is happening. And you will be moved to my apartment. I am assured that a visiting nurse or doctor can give you the injections you need." For Stefan, he was almost effervescent, but suddenly, he sobered, pursed his lips and went on, "I think the Presidium agreed because of those few minutes of silence. They can explain the engine fire as an accident, even though that can't be proved, but they are as puzzled as they're worried by the way the noise ceased. Now! You are to be given an injection to make you sleep and when you wake I hope you will be in my apartment."

Already, the English-speaking nurse was hovering, a small tray in her hand, and a doctor in a white smock was approaching her. Stefan drew back. The nurse had strong, broad-tipped fingers and a soft and gentle touch. She pushed up the sleeve of Palfrey's jacket and rubbed a spot above the bend of the elbow with alcohol, while the young doctor filled the hypodermic syringe from an ampoule which had a pink label.

The nurse held Palfrey's arm out straight, but without pressure.

She smiled.

The doctor had the needle ready, thumb on the plunger.

Then the door burst open and Philip Carr rushed in. He was wild-eyed, mouth agape. A man, just behind him, was struck by the door as it closed, and for a moment Philip was by himself in a kind of oasis of space surrounded by nurses, attendants and doctors, all near Palfrey.

"Don't do it!" Philip cried. "They'll kill you. Don't let them —"

The door swung open and two more men appeared. Philip dived towards Palfrey on the bench. The nurse tightened her grip on Palfrey's arm, and he had not the strength to resist, even had he wanted to. He was appalled by Philip's furious rush. He felt the needle when Philip was within a foot or two of the young doctor, whose face was like a mask, lips drawn back over wide-spaced teeth. The nurse was breathing gustily.

"Don't do it!" screamed Philip.

He made a grab at the doctor but ran into Stefan's outstretched arm; it was like striking a steel wall. He reeled backwards into the arms of the men just behind him. He began to struggle furiously, striking out, kicking, trying desperately to break free, and shouting words which at first had no meaning, but gradually sounded high and clear.

"Murder! It's murder! Murder!"

Palfrey felt the needle go in; a sharp pain.

He felt the nurse's firm hands on his biceps and on his wrist.

He saw the doctor wipe the sweat from his forehead.

He saw Philip being half-dragged, half-carried out of the ward, and as the door closed Stefan approached from the other side and bent over him, saying in a low-pitched earnest voice,

"It's all right, Sap. It really is all right. You need not worry."

Consciousness faded from Palfrey and he hardly heard the last words, but there was fear in him that Philip was right, that somehow the Politburo had deceived Stefan, that it was not 'all right', that he would never come round.

All about him there was blackness.

And into the room where the others still stood appalled by the outburst, shocked and not knowing what to do, came Boris Shakalov, wearing his tunic-like suit. His shaved head and pale face were startling, his eyes peculiarly bright. He approached the couch on which Palfrey lay, and asked Stefan:

"Will he recover?"

Stefan drew a deep breath, looked at him, and said, "Unless you have had him murdered."

"You are a fool," Shakalov replied acidly. "We need Palfrey as much as you do. The man who came with him appears to have that common affliction — Communist-phobia. He asked to see Palfrey, and was brought here. He did not begin to make these ludicrous accusations until he was inside the room. Do you know what is goading him, Comrade? Is he sane or is he mad?"

After a pause Stefan answered: "I would like to talk to him alone."

In a small, bare room, Philip Carr stood by one wall while Stefan sat on a hard-looking bed and looked down on the tense face, the over-bright eyes, the lips which quivered with anger. So far, Philip had not answered any of his questions, just sat mute and quivering.

"Philip, if you have a convincing reason to believe Sap's life is in danger, you must tell me. You *must*."

At last Philip said harshly, "What good will it do? Tell me — what good will it do?"

"I can perhaps help."

"If his body is full of poison, how can you help?" demanded Philip. When Stefan simply stared, knowing that if Philip did not begin to talk soon then he, Stefan Andromovitch, would have to exert pressure, possibly cause acute physical pain, Philip burst out,

"A lot of the men at The Project were Russians! I've only realised it since I've been here. And we knew some of the escape aircraft came here and others were heading for Russia on different routes. Are you such a Russian patriot that you can't see the truth even now?" He drew in a hissing breath, then he screamed, "How do you know the other aircraft didn't come here at the Kremlin's orders? How do you know it isn't a gigantic Russian conspiracy? Or *do* you know? Is that why you won't listen? *Is it*?" he screamed.

There was silence as intense as when it had been induced by The Project, except for Philip's heavy breathing. It dragged on, until it was broken by sounds outside the door, brisk footsteps on the stairs, then a peremptory knock at the door. Stefan stretched out and opened it, and Boris Shakalov came in, his movements almost militarily precise. He shot Philip one searing glance, then said to Stefan,

"I've sent word to the men of Hansa, they will allow you and Palfrey, and if you must take him, this snivelling fool, to go and see them tomorrow, Comrade. They say that if we attack in force, before or after you go, they will repeat what they did in England. They will blow their plant up with nuclear power and they will not use the insulating agent which they used in England. Radio-activity will spread all over the cities in the Urals and far, far beyond."

When he finished, he seemed to be struggling for breath, as if he already felt the tentacles of death.

17

The Men in Command

PALFREY'S RIGHT ARM was in a sling, but his leg felt almost normal, due more to the pain-killing drug than to improvement in the actual condition. He felt clear-headed, and calm. The fact that Philip was with them caused anxiety but not alarm. Once over the outburst, he had been quite rational, and had sat quietly throughout the flight from Moscow.

Stefan had hardly moved.

No-one else but the crew was with them, and nothing could have impressed Palfrey more. The leaders of The Project had said they must come alone, and they were alone. Possibly they were followed. Undoubtedly they would be watched on landing and kept under surveillance from a distance, but it would probably be at such a distance that if there were an emergency nothing could be done. The aircraft, a military passenger-carrying craft much more rough and ready than the British one had been, flew at twenty-thousand feet in a clear sky. To the west were cirrus clouds, making a curious feather-like blanket, but in all other directions the sky was clear. The sun shone in on Palfrey, who was in front of Stefan. Philip Carr was across the aisle.

It was he who looked across to Palfrey and said, unexpectedly,

"We won't be long now." And he pointed out of his window.

Palfrey crossed and leaned over him, to look out. In

the far distance, rising out of the flat land, were mountains, some of the peaks snowcapped, there was no doubt at all that these were the Urals. Below there was yellowish-brown grass, here and there a tiny cluster of buildings and a ribbon of road. Cattle and sheep were dotted about as if they were on an enormous toy farm. No city was in sight, and the flat land stretched close to the foot of the mountains.

A steward came from the gallery, a short, dark-haired man, with a very thick neck. He spoke formal English, and had brought them food and drink as well as many cups of coffee which was thick and treacly. He had not once smiled, had shown no expression of any kind. Now, he paused by Palfrey, and waited for him to turn round. The sun covered the peaks of mountains with a red glow which was reflected in the cabin and on this man's cheeks; it made him look very young.

"Yes," Palfrey smiled pleasantly.

"The captain, sir, would wish to speak to you."

"I'll come at once," Palfrey said.

There were two men at the controls and a radio-officer on one side, an engineer on the other. Palfrey saw the morning's red glow over the cockpit, and quite suddenly, he was appalled; for there was an iridescent quality about it very much the same as that on the green dust which had spread over the Midlands. The captain said something in Russian to his co-pilot, and turned away from the control panel with its dozens of switches and dials. He was very slim, with a broad nose and a slight hare-lip. He pointed to a seat hinged to a post, and as Palfrey sat down, he said:

"I am in communication with the officials of The Project, Dr. Palfrey."

"And are they giving instructions?" Palfrey asked wryly.

"That is so. There is a channel through the barrier which we can take and they will beam us down to the valley."

"Barrier," Palfrey echoed.

"They have explained that the red glow is caused by a

dust barrier to all aircraft, which will crash if they attempt to fly through," said the pilot. "I am to take off immediately you have landed."

The man at the controls cried out. The other looked round sharply. Only a short distance away, an aircraft was falling in flames from a great height; and almost on the same instant another aircraft, flying to their left, burst into flames. And as these blazing machines hurtled towards the earth, the radio-operator spoke very quickly in Russian, and the pilot translated quickly:

"They have given a demonstration of their power, Dr. Palfrey." He was obviously badly shaken. "I shall have to carry out their orders with great precision."

"Yes," Palfrey said. "You will indeed."

He went back to the cabin where Philip and Stefan sat behind the emergency exits, watching the ball of fire which had once been an aircraft, as large and solid as this. Palfrey told them what he had learned, sat down, and fastened his seat belts. The others fastened theirs. The engine noise changed as they began the descent.

Fifteen minutes later, they stood alone on the side of a hill which had a natural landing strip. All about them and on their faces was the pink glow, but no human being and no building was in sight. A few sheep nibbled at the coarse grass. A few shrubs which looked hardy and wind-blown grew about the hillside.

The noise of the aircraft which had brought them here faded into the distance.

The pink glow was no longer about them but high above their heads, almost as if a sun, buried in the earth, was bombarding the sky with tiny, iridescent particles.

Palfrey, Stefan and Philip had no weapon between them; were isolated entirely from contact with the rest of the world. Palfrey had never felt a greater sense of impending disaster; never been in such a position that all he could hope for was to talk with the leaders of The Project and try to come to terms which would be acceptable to the governments of the world.

A small aircraft appeared, almost alongside; there had been no sound of an engine, only a shadow flitting across the hillside, sending sheep scampering; and then the aircraft landed, obviously a smaller variety of the vertical take-off machines. As it stopped, as Palfrey's heart began to stop its furious thumping, doors opened and men jumped out. One of them approached, a tall, lean, fair-headed man who might develop into the image of Palfrey. His voice was that of an Englishman from a public school, pleasant, cultured, with hardly a hint of affectation.

"All aboard," he called. "Sorry if I scared you, Dr. Palfrey," but in fact he looked as if he was mildly amused.

"You might as well cut my throat as frighten me to death," Palfrey said, with grim humour. He limped towards the aircraft and was helped inside; the others followed, and in a few seconds they were taking off vertically. They did not climb very high, just followed the contours of the foot-hills, and then hovered; Palfrey saw an opening appear in the hillside, and the machine dropped down into a man-made hole.

It was like being in the bowels of a giant aircraft carrier. As they went down in a shaft large enough for aircraft twice the size of this, on either side they saw were decks, or floors, where aircraft of all shapes and sizes were being worked on; they passed at least five floors, and fifty aircraft, perhaps five hundred men, before they reached a 'deck' which had only desks and computers and control panels, not unlike that at the headquarters of Z5.

The aircraft stopped.

On all sides, now, was a kind of quayside buried in the mountainside; there were small cars, cycles, aircraft, trains; and obviously each was driven by electricity, they were so quiet and moved so slowly. The quays led to brightly-lit tunnels, like highways leading from a great hub. Palfrey was helped out and into a small open car which had four seats but no driver. Philip and Stefan were also ushered in, and the pilot said:

"You will be taken to the Leaders, Dr. Palfrey."

The car moved off, without any visible sign of power or engine. It ran smoothly, as if on a cushion of air, but without any of the roaring of hovercraft. It turned along narrow tunnels, all well-lit. There were other cars, on a track which ran parallel, and ahead of and behind this one. Every few hundred yards they passed platforms or loading bays, at each of which they slowed down.

At one, they stopped; and men in dark trousers and pale grey turtle-neck sweaters came to help them out. They were led to narrow doors which opened as they approached and then into a room not unlike Shakalov's, except that this was smaller. There was a crescent-shaped table with six chairs around, and three chairs in front. They were ushered to these seats, and waited.

Philip said thinly, "Psychological terrorism, Sap."

"I'm not terrified yet," Palfrey remarked.

"Believe me, *I* am," said Philip.

The words were hardly out of his mouth when a door behind the crescent opened and a man stepped through, followed by another and another, six in all. They took chairs at the crescent-shaped table, like the judges at a court martial or the courts of appeal.

Six in all —

The first man looked *exactly* like the President of the United States.

The second was the living image of the British Prime Minister.

The third was the double of the President of the U.S.S.R.

The fourth was the double of the President of the Republic of China, Mao.

The fifth was like the President of India.

The sixth was like the recently elected Secretary-General of the United Nations Association — Oboku.

Each of the six sat down.

Each of the six smiled.

The last man, so like Oboku, raised his right hand and said in his deep and arresting voice:

"You are very welcome, gentlemen. We are as anxious as you to find a way to peace, and we have invited you here because you have already learned of our basic plan, and it seems possible that you are the men most likely to be able to bridge the gap between us and the nations of the world. There is little point in wasting time, since there is so much fear and uncertainty, and so much emphasis on the preparations for war when the world is in such desperate need of peace. So: you already know much; and may have guessed more. You may even have guessed that we have not yet perfected all our technologies. *Silence* was to have surrounded your aircraft on arrival, but the fire was not intended." He raised his hands. "After our experience of you in London and England and the readiness with which the real Mr. Wetherall as well as other national leaders have responded to you, we want to work with you. So let us tell you at once what we propose to do." He paused and smiled very freely, a startlingly handsome negro. "It is very simple. Each of us has studied the leaders of the nations you see represented here. Each of us proposes to impersonate a national leader. Once we are at the helm of our respective nations, we propose slowly to alter the course of affairs, so that we have basically world government instead of national government." He paused, and then asked with his beaming smile, "Isn't that your chief objective also, Dr. Palfrey?"

Palfrey said quietly, "Yes, Dr. Oboku."

"Can you tell us with any confidence that the world which you represent is on the threshold of an understanding; will switch almost immediately from a war orientation to a wholly peaceful one?"

"No," Palfrey admitted. "I cannot claim this."

"Then is there any reason why you should not work with us?"

Palfrey hesitated, battling with an aspect of the situation which hadn't occurred to him when he had arrived. These men might believe that he had already discovered their fundamental purpose *and* their identities; yet he had had no knowledge of these at all. What had made them so ready to bring about this meeting?

He opened his lips to speak, but Philip spoke first in a passionate voice, revealing anger which seethed inside him.

"There are a hundred reasons! A thousand. And the first one is that you will impose your bloody laws, you will dictate to the people, not consult them."

"Dr. Palfrey," Oboku said in a rather patronising way, "do you and your agents really adhere to these outworn concepts of democracy?"

"We — " began Palfrey.

"They're no more outworn than breathing is!" Philip cried. His face had gone pale, there seemed no difference between the colour of his lips and of his cheeks. "You don't even begin to understand, you're dealing with men, with human beings, not with machines or mindless creatures. Before I would allow Palfrey or Andromovitch to do a deal with you I would kill them."

Oboku's smile grew broader.

"And how do you respond to that? Dr. Palfrey?"

"I want to know what you propose," Palfrey said.

"Andromovitch?"

"I would like to hear what you have to say," Stefan replied.

"You mean, you will consider betraying everything you're supposed to stand for — everything you're supposed to believe in?" Philip shouted. "Haven't you *seen* what these men have done, how they've tortured, slaughtered, spread radio-active dust over big cities? My God, I could cut your throats!"

"Philip," murmured Palfrey, "you are contradicting everything you were saying only two days ago."

"I wanted to try to find out what you were really made of, and now I know. You didn't fool me, even then. When I pretended to believe in the benefits these megalomaniacs might bring to the world I could see what was going through your mind. You *agreed* with me. You argued but in your heart you agreed. And if you had your way you would come to terms with murderers, with tyrants who would trample on freedom. You can't imprison the minds of people without destroying freedom and if you destroy that you destroy man himself. I thought you knew! I joined Z5 because I thought you were the one man who would always fight tyranny and dictatorship. Why, I could strangle you with my bare hands."

In a low-pitched voice, Oboku said: "I should not try."

"You know you are being very childish," said the man who looked so like Wetherall, and now proved to speak in a voice startlingly similar to the Prime Minister's. "You yourself would have freedom, Carr. Freedom from fear and want, freedom to worship as you wished, freedom to love — "

He paused, with a touch of drama in his manner; and on the instant the door behind the crescent-shaped table opened, and a woman came into the room.

She was Jane Wylie.

There was no shadow of doubt about her identity; and she looked at her loveliest and in glowing health.

She moved forward as all the men at the table stood up and smiled at her as at an old friend.

Then she went towards Philip Carr with her hands outstretched.

His arms went slowly out towards her, but there was anguish in his face, anguish in his manner when their fingers were almost touching. Palfrey and Andromovitch were acutely aware of her attractiveness and, even more, of her serenity.

Suddenly, Philip snatched his hands away.

"Don't come near me!" he cried. "Don't touch me." And as her expression changed to one of ludicrous dismay, he went on: "There is no freedom if man is compelled to do what others want him to."

Janey stood very still.

Philip, quivering from head to foot, stood in front of his chair.

"Gentlemen," said Oboku, "what is needed is a little time."

"What you have to understand," the Russian impersonator said, "is that your methods, Dr. Palfrey, are no better than ours. Haven't *you* torture chambers? Don't you control the minds of men when you think it's for the common good? Don't you use force and strategy, cunning and deceit to get what you think right?"

Palfrey, who could not say 'no', did not respond at all.

"And Palfrey," said the man who could have convinced the world, by voice as well as by appearance, that he was the President of the United States. "You have to remember and Carr has to realise that by the time-honoured — or should I say time dishonoured? — democratic methods, the world is a cauldron of conflict, and a dust-bowl in which millions starve? Isn't that true?"

"Dr. Palfrey," said the man who looked so like the President of China, "is it not better that a man should be compelled to behave with goodness rather than allowed, even encouraged, to be bad?"

And Palfrey stayed silent, aware of Stefan's absolute stillness, and Carr's quivering, and the woman's serenity.

"Dr. Palfrey," said the man who could have convinced the world that he was the newly elected President of India, "my people starve. Should we not compel the world to feed them? For we do not lack the means, only the will."

And Palfrey bowed his head.

"Palfrey," said the man who was impersonating Wetherall: "You are the one man trusted by the world's leaders. If you call a meeting of all the leaders of the nations represented ere — in London, in Moscow, in Washington, anywhere — hey will come. And we will replace them, one by one. You an render the greatest service to mankind."

"None will be harmed," Oboku put in gently.

"But if you will not work with us," 'Wetherall' said, 'millions will be harmed. We would far rather win by subtlety than by violence, but we do have the means to get victory one way or the other. You have seen so many examples of our power. We can use the crystals, powdered crystals of great variety, to insulate the air against sound — against radio-activity. We have evolved rays which can be used as rockets to bring down aircraft, to sink great ships. We can create great areas which are safe from pollution as well as from contamination. In the process armies and air forces and navies will be pitted against us, but they cannot succeed, for we can approach them in the stealth of our silence, creep up on them with weapons of incalculable destructive power.

"And you can prevent the carnage, Palfrey. You can save the world. I doubt if any other man can."

18

Time of Decision

THE LAST WORDS fell gently. No-one in the room moved, even Philip's trembling had ceased, and he was looking at 'Wetherall' with hopelessness in his eyes. He avoided Jane Wylie's gaze. All the men at the crescent-shaped table were looking at Palfrey as if no-one else was in the room.

Still he did not speak.

He heard Stefan move, draw a deep breath, and say, "We need time to consider, time to think."

Oboku looked along the men alongside him.

"Is that reasonable?" he asked.

Each man nodded, or said 'yes' in turn, while staring at Palfrey. And he was agonisingly aware of their gaze, of the weight of responsibility which they had thrust upon him.

"How long?" asked Oboku.

"Twelve hours at least," Stefan answered quietly, and he looked at Palfrey. "Is that long enough, Sap?"

Palfrey moistened his lips but did not answer. He studied each of the men in front of him in turn, then turned to Jane Wylie until her gaze shifted towards him; she looked startled, almost afraid. He turned away from her and spoke at last, to Oboku.

"What made you so sure I knew what you were doing?" he asked.

"Made us so sure?" echoed Oboku, and shot a startled

look at Jane Wylie. "We were told so. Did you not know we had been informed?"

"Ah," Palfrey said. "Who told you?"

"But Sap," Jane Wylie interrupted. "*I* told them. Who else could?" She moved towards him, now. "You always told me, as an agent of Z5, that I should hold out to the limit of my resistance, and only then give way. I *did* hold out; but at last I had to tell them I worked for Z5, that I had been able to send out a great deal of other information and was quite sure other agents had, too. I tried to make them realise that if there was any hope of avoiding world disaster, they had to confer with you."

Every man in the room was hanging on to her words, none more than Palfrey, and he was so intent that he did not even wonder what Philip Carr was thinking.

He, Palfrey, was the only man in the room who knew that she was lying; knew that she was not a member of Z5 and never had been. But she had convinced these men that she was.

What an agent she would be!

And how much they owed to her, for whatever chance there remained.

He raised his uninjured hand and gestured with the other.

"There will never be another agent like you," he declared; and he was almost sure there was a spark of humour in her eyes.

"Gentlemen," interrupted Oboku, quietly, "it is agreed that you should have not twelve but twenty-four hours in which to consider your decision. We shall now adjourn. We hope you will all join us for dinner, and after that you will be able to sleep on your deliberations. We shall expect you to tell us what you have decided here, tomorrow, at this time."

He stood up, bowed slightly, and went out, and the others filed after him. Another door opened, and two men and two women stood in a room set for a buffet breakfast, with bacon and eggs and sausages on hot-plates, some buckwheat cakes and maple syrup, coffee, tea, cocoa and chocolate.

Leading off this were washrooms and beyond these, singl
bedrooms rather like those in a good quality motel or hotel
The three men washed, Palfrey with some difficulty, and
went back to the room which had off-white walls with the
flags of all the world's nations, in wooden panels about it
Jane was still there, and there was some constraint between
her and Philip although much less than there had been. They
sat at a table for four, served with quiet efficiency, and
lingered over coffee — good, creamy American coffee.

A man in a turtle-neck sweater came in with a letter for
Palfrey. He opened it, read, and turned it so that the others
could see. It read:

When you are ready you may go, if you wish, to a patio
above ground, where the day will be pleasantly warm
and where you may talk without fear of being overheard
                                              Joku Oboku

Even the signature was identical with the real man's!

"Do you know," Stefan said in a reflective voice, "I could
grow to like that man."

"I don't know whether I ought to admit it, but I've come
to like them all," said Janey. She looked at Philip apprehen-
sively, as she went on: "And I've come to admire and respect
them, too."

"They *must* be wrong!" cried Philip.

Palfrey didn't respond, and Stefan finished his coffee and
then stood up to his full height.

"We are all wrong, some of the time." His tone changed.
"I would like a bath and an hour's rest before we go up to
the surface. Would that suit you, Sap?"

"Very well indeed," said Palfrey.

They went to their adjoining rooms, where Palfrey found
a man in a white smock waiting, a Chinese who spoke in
good if patchy English.

"I am to help you, sir, and also dress your burns," he
said. "We have in communication been with the doctors in

Moscow and we know what is the best to treat. It will not be necessary to give you a local anaesthetic, today, the drugs which heal are most remarkable. No?" He went on chattering as he gave Palfrey a sponge bath on the bed, and Palfrey's thoughts drifted from this man and his brightness, marvelling at the trouble that had been taken over him, trying not to think too much about Janey and the brilliant way she had convinced these men that she worked for Z5, trying desperately to come to grips with the problem.

What should he do?

The firm hands massaged him; the sound of flesh moving over flesh, the occasional slap, a kind of rhythm, went through his body and, it seemed, through his mind. What should he do? Which course was the right one? Was it right to allow the world to go on as it was doing? *Look at the facts.* There were sickness, pollution, hatred and greed. There was envy, cruelty and malice. Crime was rife in every country, even in those where social standards were good and few if any were hungry. The moral standards which had lasted for centuries were breaking, yes, but — had they been the right ones? Was it time they broke down? Wave after wave of eroticism, of drug-taking, of promiscuity followed each other. Whole generations, it seemed whole nations, succumbed to them. The family as a family was being broken up, derided and despised and rejected. There had never been such a complete breakdown of accepted standards, since the days of Nero's Rome.

'Love' had become a word used simply to mean sexual intercourse; 'love' as a permanent feeling was gone.

Such as his for his wife, Drusilla...

Oh, God! How the loss of her hurt, even today.

Love was not a fleeting thing, the old standards, traditions and habits *were* gone. In wars between nations other nations supplied the warring groups and gained more profit from the war than from the peace. Civil wars could divide a nation, whole tribes, whole races threatened with extinction while powerful nations stood aside and washed their hands in the way of Pontius Pilate.

What was the use of fighting for good if the bad was so often triumphant?

What was the use of fighting for the freedom of man's mind if man himself enslaved that mind by drugs or drink, or else destroyed the freedom by turning it into licence, abusing all that the great men and the meek men of the ages had wrested from the tyrant and the weakling kings.

How right was he to continue to fight for the old gods?

And conversely, how wrong were men like the impersonators he had seen and talked to? Men who had contrived to control power by violence and deception, and who argued so speciously, even convincingly, for imposed goodness, not goodness won out of the blood and the slaughter and the starvation and the slavery of the centuries.

Here were men who *had* power and had demonstrated it; and these same men in the high places of authority could say to the world: *"Do good, or you shall perish."*

Was it, faced so coldly, different from the old laws?

Was it so different from the Commandments of the prophets — even, he thought in anguish, from Christ?

Were these new holders of power the true gods or the false?

These were the questions that formed in his mind and turned over and over in it as the firm hands moulded and pushed and pinched and slapped the flesh.

At last, the masseur said, "All finish now, sir. I help off table?" His small arm was like steel. He gave Palfrey another gentle rub and then rebandaged the leg, which had healed much better than he had dared to hope. It was still tender to the touch and he had to put his foot down gingerly, but the rest of his body glowed with well-being.

"You're a man of magic fingers," he declared.

"Very grateful for compliment," the man replied. "It is easy to make magic in magic place. Now — " he helped Palfrey on with a lightweight jacket taken from some unseen wardrobe. "I see if Mr. Andellivich ready, yes? To go up to patio and bathe the sun, eh?"

Stefan, wearing his own jacket and trousers, also looked as if he too were glowing with health. At this realisation, Palfrey caught his breath. Apart from his wounds, he had never felt better. Jane Wylie looked as if she had just come off a health farm. Stefan, pale and troubled until now, had a clear complexion and clear eyes; he was the picture of health, as if all the fatigue and the anxiety had been drawn out of him. These thoughts were vivid in Palfrey's mind as he walked towards the closed glass doors of an elevator, which opened as they approached.

The masseur bowed.

"Good appetites," he said. "I hope to see again."

The doors closed. They had an immediate sense of movement in the softly lighted cage but could not see through the walls of the elevator. Stefan was studying Palfrey as if he, too, were aware of something different. There was the faintest sensation of slowing down, and then the doors opened silently on to a world of sunlit beauty, as if it were touched with heaven. Awestruck, Palfrey stepped out on to a paved terrace, beyond which were waist-high wrought-iron railings, but he was oblivious of these aware only of the vista. It stretched into illimitable distances beyond twin peaks, each snowcapped and brilliant in the sunshine.

Like silver crystals . . .

Beyond these peaks mountains seemed to spill, each range more magnificent than the other, each with its own colouring and its trees, its shapes and its sharp outline. He had seen such views only two or three times, in Wyoming, in the Himalayas, in Switzerland; but none surpassed this.

He went forward very slowly, staring out, until Stefan joined him.

"Have you never been here before?" he asked.

"Never," said Palfrey. "It's beyond words to describe." He gulped. "Have *you* been here before?"

"In a place like it, during the war. There were some

Germans up here, showing the aircraft the way to the big industrial belts of the Urals, and I was one who had to seek them out. It was only a few months before we first met, Sap. And that seems a lifetime ago."

Palfrey made himself turn away from the vista, and say in a baffled way, not intending to be facetious:

"Only one lifetime?"

Stefan shrugged, "Sometimes it has seemed a dozen."

"And the past few days a lifetime in itself. Do you feel like that, too?"

"Yes," Stefan answered. "Sap — " there was a shadow on his face despite the wholesomeness, the glow of health; his eyes were slightly narrowed, his hands raised in front of his chest as if he were trying to use gestures to explain what words alone could not say. "Sap, are you at the crossroads?"

"Yes," Palfrey responded. "I didn't think I could ever be, but I am."

"So here we are," Stefan said, and after a long pause, went on, "And we have to go one way or the other." He put a hand at Palfrey's elbow and led him away from the twin peaks and the view which might so easily be of Shangri-La, and then towards a narrow passage alongside a covered patio. "Jane Wylie told me to come here," he said, and opened a tall wooden gate which was on a latch. He stepped aside to allow Palfrey to pass, and Palfrey saw yet another range of mountains.

These were in shadow, for the sun was behind the snow-capped peaks. And they were dark, almost black, as if this were the scene of some volcanic eruption which had left only devastation in its wake. Beyond these nearer slopes were others just as dark; sulphurous. Palfrey hesitated then went on, towards a gap between two peaks on which was stunted, blackened vegetation. There was a vista beyond the peaks, of darkness and smoke, of fires, like the blazing of great lakes of oil. Near him was a telescope, one fitted to a pedestal as at a seaside resort or on a mountain overlook where many people went to gaze into the valleys. Almost as if he was acting under some strange compulsion, Palfrey bent his head and put his eye to the glass. It was already focused.

He seemed to be looking down at hell. There was great factories, chimneys belching fire and smoke; there were huge steelworks; there were rows upon rows of tiny blackened houses. There were cranes and derricks working, huge lines of railways trucks, waiting to be filled, workers by the thousand who worked as if they were slaves.

Then out of the floor on which Palfrey stood came Joku Oboku's voice, very quietly but unmistakably.

"That is today's world. You see but a picture, but it is the world our generation is making: poisoned air, poisoned rivers, poisoned oceans, corrupted minds. Which way are you going to choose, Palfrey?" And, as if he could see the expression on Palfrey's face he went on with a soft laugh. "You have to make the choice, you know, and make it for mankind. Where are you going to lead them, Palfrey? To bright heaven or dark hell?"

When Palfrey did not answer, the other man went on, "If you still have doubts, let me re-create the sounds you hear. It will be from a sound-track but you will recognise each one and know that it is the kind of sound which is possessing the earth."

19

To Heaven or to Hell

OBOKU'S VOICE FADED, and Stefan stood close to Palfrey's side. As they stared out over the pictures of dark valleys, a sound began, coming from the spot where Oboku's voice had been. It was at first distant and confused, but gradually it became a throb; of great generators working, of pistons thrusting, furnaces roaring, machines clattering, whistles piercing, steam hissing. And all of these grew louder, and added to them were great crashing sounds, as of cars smashing into one another at high speed, of trains hurtling, of tanks rumbling.

The air about the platform seemed to shudder with the din.

Other sounds followed.

A siren, wailing — people, screaming — the unmistakable crashing of exploding bombs — the rattle of machine guns and of rifle fire, of mortars and grenades.

And women, crying.

And children, wailing.

All these noises merged together in one horrendous cacophony. Each sound was distinct and recognisable yet all of them merged together made a great roaring and rushing; as if the earth itself were hurtling out of its orbit into space. The ground on which they stood began to tremble as if the eye of this maelstrom of noise was not out in the distance but close by, beneath them.

Palfrey felt Stefan's hand on his shoulder. Neither moved, except with the vibrating earth. And as their bodies shook so did their minds, until the screaming and the wailing seemed to come not from the bowels of the earth but from their heads; a concentrated fury of sound not only deafening but tearing their brain cells apart.

Nothing was still.

The near mountains were blurred in indefinable outline, there were no shapes except moving ones, above and all around them. The hand on Palfrey's shoulder pressed in like a steel claw, harder and harder.

Suddenly, Palfrey cried, "Stop it! Stop!"

He wrenched himself free and glared at Stefan, and saw Stefan's eyes closed and his great body hunched as if he were trying to fight away the noise, the horror of it all. Stefan's face quivered, his body shook, as Palfrey's was shaking, but his mouth was set as if it were a trap.

"Stop it!" cried Palfrey. "Stop!"

On the instant the noise fell away to silence and the quivering fell away to stillness. His head and his body ached but slowly the aching eased. Stefan opened his eyes and his mouth slackened; all the glow of health had gone from him and there was sweat on his forehead and greyness on his cheeks.

Oboku's voice sounded with its reassuring warmth.

"Walk back to the patio, Dr. Palfrey. It is much more peaceful there."

Palfrey took Stefan's arm and they turned their backs on the valleys of turmoil and walked, very slowly, to the patio where they had first come. Here the sun shone, pleasantly warm. A child laughed; a man chuckled; a woman gave a sigh as of contentment. There was more, distant laughter, the sound of a cascading waterfall; a choirboy, singing; and far distant the sound of a jazz drummer playing as if his heart and soul as well as his hands and arms, his whole body, were obsessed by the joy of his playing.

Two comfortable-looking chairs stood near the rail, and they sat down. The sounds ceased but the new look of tranquility remained and the tension eased out of their bodies. From behind them a Vietnamese girl appeared, wearing long trousers and the long ribbons of cloth which half-concealed them. Smiling but saying nothing, she placed coffee in a china pot, cups and saucers, some orange juice with sugar, and a bowl of fruit on a table between the two chairs. When she had done, her smile became broader and her face prettier as she spread both hands towards the sun-drenched vista, which was still lovely although some of the colour had been drawn out by the sun.

She went off, and the two men were alone; the leader of Z5 and his deputy. That was the moment when Palfrey realised that neither Janey nor Philip was here; it was as if he and Stefan were together and alone on top of the world. It was pleasantly warm, and he sipped the ice-cold orange juice. Already, he felt calmer and already Stefan looked better. It was as if this side of the mountain was an elixir of life, inducing a sense of well-being. Stefan poured himself coffee, and as he was sipping, the lift doors opened and Jane Wylie called.

"Good morning. No, please don't get up." She hurried to stop Palfrey from rising, and waved Stefan back to his chair. She wore a primrose yellow dress with short sleeves, cut round at the neck and rather low, and a hem which fell just below the knee. It was not the latest but certainly not a dated fashion. She moved freely, drawing up a stool and sitting in front of them. As she leaned forward her bosom showed, and the gleam in her eyes suggested that was intended. "How are you both?" she asked.

"Pensive," answered Palfrey.

"Inevitably," said Stefan.

"Not despairing?"

"Not yet," replied Palfrey.

"Sap," she said, leaning forward still further and putting out her hands. She used his name as if she were thoroughly familiar with it, and her eyes positively danced. "It's like heaven up here. Shall I tell you a naughty secret?"

She sounded not only gay but childlike.

And she was pressing some papers into his hand as she held him tightly.

"I would love to hear a naughty secret," Palfrey declared.

Soon, very soon, he had to make the most vital decision of his life; but he could talk lightly, even facetiously with her. He palmed the paper and, while she still held his hands, worked it up to his wrist and under the sleeve of his shirt.

"This place is heavenly for a honeymoon."

"What's naughty about honeymoons?"

She was half-laughing with her eyes, and half-pleading.

"They should come *after* the wedding!" She leaned further forward so that all he could see was her face; and the glowing and the pleading in her eyes. "Sap — I love Philip so."

"And Philip loves you," Palfrey replied, gently.

"Yes, I think he does."

"So, your honeymoon anticipates the wedding. Is that unique?" Stefan asked.

She glanced at him.

"No," she replied. "No. Sap — I want to get away from here. I don't want to have to stay here all my life, even with Philip. *We* want to get away. I — I hate talking like this but I can't help myself."

He had the paper unfolded, now; all he had to do was shift its position so that he could read it as he looked down at her. His heart was beating very fast. He was sure they were watched and that she was aware of it, or she would not have smuggled the message, would not be acting so as to give him a chance of reading it.

"Go on," he urged.

"Sap," she said, "do what they ask you."

He didn't reply.

"Sap, I beg you," she went on, and now he could see tears glistening in her eyes. "Do what they want. Then they'll let Philip and me go back to the world. If you don't, they'll keep us here."

He seemed to be staring into her eyes, and now there was no doubt about the tears; nor of the strength in her hands, reflecting her tension. He eased the paper on to his leg, so that he could read the few words written there in black ink.

"Sap, please — " she was sobbing now.

He read:

They are watching, listening, everywhere. There is a path beyond the railing, your only possible way of escape . . .

So what she was saying was simply to deceive them; she really wanted him and Stefan to try to escape; so, she was still utterly opposed to the leaders of The Project.

He read on:

Philip is a prisoner — a surety for me. But never mind us. Escape while you can. They don't believe in freedom except for the rulers. They are the worst of tyrants, and even the highest skilled workers are slaves.

"Sap," she said, fighting back tears which seemed as real as her gaiety had a few minutes before. "Philip and I can marry and live in peace. And the leaders of The Project *can* control atomic power and atomic radio-activity and noise. They have perfected the manufacture of tiny crystals which can be used as insulators, and if they wish, conveyors. The green crystals cancel out the radio-activity, the pink crystals create a barrier nothing can pass; anything which comes in contact with it disintegrates. They can use them like invisible rays, too; or as rockets which make no sound. They can do everything they say, and if you oppose them then they will simply crush all opposition, destroy great cities — Sap!" she cried. "There is no way of stopping them, you must work with them."

Now, her lips quivered and tears spilled. As he palmed the note again, sliding it this time into his shirt cuff. She went on:

"It — it isn't just Philip and me. It isn't just that we want to get married and live together. It will be a better life for all who submit. There will be no hunger left, nor fear, nor ignorance — "

She broke off, placing her hands together in an attitude of prayer, and after a long time continued in a voice from which all strength had been drained.

"You can't prevent them taking over, you can only make it easy, free from slaughter and the maiming of war. Work with them, *please*."

They are tyrants, and even the most skilled workers are slaves.

Living slaves; happy, healthy slaves?
Or dead, despairing, sick 'free' men?
How should the people be?

"Stefan," Palfrey said, hoarsely.

"Yes, Sap?" It was remarkable how Stefan could give significance to remarks or words which in themselves were trite.

"What do you think we should do?"

"I think we should accept the offer," Stefan answered, simply.

"Out of hand?"

"Of course," Stefan said. "Don't you believe that, now?"

"I'm still not sure," Palfrey answered slowly. "Why are you?"

Stefan answered quietly: "In the past we had a chance of winning without avoidable bloodshed; or at least we had a chance of winning. Now we cannot possibly win. We can only bring about unthinkable bloodshed. It isn't possible to take the responsibility for all people, we have no right to do it. Our only course is to agree and, when these men have taken over, help them to run the world without pain or hardship. The principles will remain. We shall be able to live by them and help others to live by them as well."

His expression was so earnest, his face so saint-like, there seemed no doubt at all that he meant exactly what he said.

And Janey watched him with awed fascination, as he echoed all that she had said and rejected everything she had written. Palfrey put his hands on her elbows and eased her back, and she stood up, still crying. He left her and moved towards the wrought-iron railing and looked across at the sunlit hills and the snowcapped mountains and the distant valleys. No-one moved or spoke but Oboku's voice seemed to echo in his mind: *"Where are you going to lead them, Palfrey? To bright heaven or to dark hell?"*

Then Oboku's voice *did* sound:

"There it is, Dr. Palfrey. There *is* the promised land."

The awful thing was that the decision would be forced on him. By doing nothing he could unleash the dogs of war. By keeping silent, saying nothing, then he and Stefan would be condemned to stay here, like Janey and Philip, until the battles were fought and the end had come. Slowly, man would have to rebuild the shattered world.

He saw a movement some way down the mountainside, thought that it was a sheep, stared again because he saw it was a man, climbing between boulders and up a narrow path, little more than a defile between overhanging rocks. Stefan joined him, and stared; and whispered:

"It's Zuka."

"Are you sure?"

"It's Zuka," Stefan repeated. "Sap — "

"Read this," Palfrey whispered, and held the note so that both could read. He did not think there was any fear of being watched or overheard, for there was a sheer drop from the railing into a valley, and there were no walls in which a microphone could be built.

No wall?

There was the railing.

He glanced along this, as Stefan read in silence, and saw a tiny grille not more than a foot away. He half-laughed at himself for his brief folly, and moved, gripped the railing on either side of the microphone and then, as if by chance placed a hand over it.

"We can stay here and keep silent," he said, "or we can go. Did you mean what you said or was it for the listener-in?"

"I meant it," Stefan said. "I can't accept the responsibility for allowing the kind of war they will undoubtedly fight." He was quite calm, and his voice was steady. "I don't think Janey would write like this if she knew the consequences. Sap, I wish to God I hadn't to reach a decision, I wish you hadn't either."

"I know," Palfrey said. "I know."

He broke off, for Zuka, hidden until that moment by an outcrop of pale grey rocks, appeared again quite near the railing. He stood still and waved; and waved again; and when neither of them moved he bent his knees and spread his arms wide and then raised them sharply and straightened his knees. He repeated the movement three times, then rose to his full height and beckoned furiously.

"What does he mean?" Stefan asked.

"Who is it?" Janey had joined Palfrey on the other side.

"He's telling us the mountainside is going to blow up," Palfrey said in a chokey voice. "What else can he mean?"

There were footsteps on the patio, and Philip Carr came hurrying, crying out in a loud voice:

"The valley's subsiding on the other side."

"Come down here!" cried Zuka. "Hearrr!" His voice echoed.

"Come on!" exclaimed Philip, and as he spoke he lifted Janey up bodily and swung her over the railing, where there was a narrow ledge. He vaulted the railing, put an arm round her waist, and hustled her along.

"Sap," Stefan said in a strangled voice, "we haven't any choice now, we've got to try to escape." He placed his great hands on Palfrey's waist and hoisted Palfrey over the railing. Ahead, the others were scrambling down the hillside, and as Palfrey and Stefan followed there was a great roar of sound, and the earth shook in a terrible paroxysm. Palfrey glanced over his shoulder, and saw the top of the patio building disappearing on the far side of the peak. Rocks began to roll. He was almost oblivious of the pain in his left leg now, but still had to lean on Stefan.

Janey and Philip passed Zuka, who pointed downwards; and when Palfrey and Stefan reached him he said in broken English:

"That trail — quick, quick. That one!" He pointed to a narrow gap between two rocks, as the other two disappeared into it. There was another great explosion beneath their feet, and the earth seemed to sink, but it did not go far. Rocks came tumbling, but as Palfrey reached the gap he saw that a narrow trail led upwards to another peak, not downwards; and no boulders fell.

It was as if a giant hand were shaking the earth, until suddenly they were in the defile where the shaking grew much less. Protecting peaks rose almost sheer above them, but from the patio and the valley from whence they had come there came roar upon roar, and the tops of the mountains began to cave in and fill up the centre of the valley.

In the valley itself the earth seemed to seethe in frustrated fury, some fighting to come up, but the great weight falling, filling up the valley, so that the full force of the explosions was felt below ground.

20

The Power of the Silence

SOON, THERE WAS a wider track, and by it two small land-rover type vehicles, each with two Russian soldiers. A great cloud covered the peaks behind them and there was a constant shower of small stones and rocks. One of the soldiers came hurrying with a stack of steel helmets, and Palfrey slammed one on as the shower grew thicker and the rocks larger. They bundled into the vehicles and the four-wheel drive made the going over rock-strewn mountain-side comparatively easy. Stefan was squeezed against one side, Palfrey wedged between him and the other door. The jolting hurt both injured leg and injured hand, but neither caused great pain. Soon, they entered another, lower valley, and then a camp with wooden buildings, some tanks, more land-rovers, barrels of oil, every kind of store. This was at the foot of a green-clad hill where sheep grazed and everything seemed peaceful. The vehicles drew up outside a long, low building, and as Palfrey began to get out, Shakalov appeared, in a fur-collared greatcoat and astrakhan hat which made it look as if he were wearing a wig.

He was smiling very broadly.

"You are a welcome sight," he said. "We did not think you would escape. If there are any angels, Dr. Palfrey, they are certainly on your side."

"Did you blow the mountain up?" asked Palfrey, limping into the building.

"If by 'we' you mean the Russian authorities — yes and no," answered Shakalov. When Palfrey simply looked at him, with obvious disfavour, he went on, "We mined and prepared the area for the explosion from many miles away, all the openings hidden in the sides of the mountains. There was a small experimental rocket station through which the materials were sent. But we consulted other Governments including yours before making the final decision. We were convinced that there was only this one hiding-place left, and that if the wind blew to the east after a nuclear blast it could wipe out the whole of the Ural industrial and residential areas. This morning the wind will drive it only into desolate, uninhabited mountains and valleys. And the other Governments agreed it was the time to act. Wouldn't you have advised them to, Palfrey?"

Palfrey said heavily: "I'm not sure. I think, yes." He was aware of Janey and Philip, watching. "But no — I am not sure."

"Then I am very glad you did not have to make the decision. What would you have done, Comrade Andromovitch?"

"I think I would have co-operated with the leaders of The Project," answered Stefan.

"So, such differences of opinion between men who are usually so much in accord," observed Shakalov. He was in a hearty and expansive mood. "I am even more glad you did not have to decide!" He turned to the man who had led them to the vehicles, a short, stocky man in a blanket-jacket and big knee boots. "You know Comrade Zuka, of course."

Palfrey said: "We met once." He shook hands.

"We are old friends," said Stefan, and he seemed almost to wrench the other man's arm off. "And we need some explanation, please."

"It is easy," Zuka said. "I observed over a period of months the unusual activity in the valley, but thought it was

Russian activity and that there was no need to report to Z5."
He had dark, nervy eyes, rather like tree-ripened olives. "It
is no part of my duty to Z5 to report on military or industrial
activity in the country."

"No," murmured Palfrey.

"But others had observed and reported it, and it was found
not to originate from Russian sources," put in Shakalov. "So
we built observation posts by burrowing through the moun-
tainsides. Once we knew what was beneath the valley, it was
a simple matter to take explosives and to fill it in so that the
radio-activity would be kept below ground. You see, Dr.
Palfrey, we had no difficulty in deciding."

"No," Palfrey said. You also buried the secret of the
crystals; the way these men could cut out sound and decon-
taminate radio-active areas."

"Finding these things is simply a matter of time," Shakalov
said, airily. "If your researchers don't soon find a way, ours
will. Eh, Mr. Carr?"

Philip, standing now with Stefan on one side and Jane on
the other, pursed his lips, and deliberated before saying:

"It could take a very long time."

"It could take far too long," Jane Wylie put in, quietly.
"Sap, I know I could have been wrong, but I was never in
doubt from the time I realised who you were and whom
Philip represented. They — the people of The Project,
showed me your photograph and asked me to say whether I
knew you. At first I said I didn't, but slowly it dawned on
me that it might be more valuable if I said yes, I worked
for you and Z5. Directly I claimed this, they changed their
attitude, helped me all they could, somehow made me feel
better than I've ever felt in my life. But — I *did* see the
slaves."

"They actually used whips to force some workers to work
harder," Philip said. "They had tomorrow in their hands,
and they lived in yesterday."

"Sap," said Janey, "you still seem doubtful."

"In a way I am," Palfrey admitted. "All of the good of the future is built on the iniquities of the past." He seemed to frown for a long time but then at last he shrugged. "But in the end I didn't have to choose, thank God!"

"Which was very good," said Stefan. He gave a funny little laugh. "What is it you say in English? Silence is golden."

Shakalov began to smile, Zuka chuckled. Philip threw up his hands as if in resignation. Stefan gripped Palfrey's arm for a moment, and Janey slid her hand into his good one. Almost at once a large helicopter landed to pick them up, and soon they were in a small jet passenger aircraft, roaring along a military runway.

It was nearly dark when they approached Moscow, and the lights of the city made a wonderland, reflecting in the wide river, showing up the great squares. They landed at the Moscow Airport, and Shakalov said to Palfrey:

"You are most welcome to stay the night, or for several days."

"You're very kind," said Palfrey, "but I ought to get back. May we catch the first commercial flight to London?"

"I shall need some discussions with Andromovitch, so he must stay," said Shakalov, "but you need have no fear, Comrade. We are more than ever persuaded of the value of Z5, whether it is very vocal or very quiet. I hope you will come and spend some time here, before long."

"I should like that very much," Palfrey replied, sounding quite humble.

"Sap," said Janey when he had gone and while Stefan and Philip were talking together. "I was right, wasn't I?"

He looked at her solemnly, and then replied:

"To do what you did, a million times. In what you wanted me to do — I can only tell you what I told Shakalov: I'm honestly not sure. What I *am* sure —" he broke off.

"Yes?"

"That we're back in the world as it was and have to make the best of it," Palfrey finished drily.

"How right you are!" cried Janey, so warmly that Stefan and Philip turned to look at them. "Sap —"

"Yes?"

"Can I help?"

He chuckled, "Become a member of Z5 retrospectively, you mean?"

"There's nothing I would like more."

"Philip might have other ideas," Palfrey said.

"I don't think he will," retorted Janey. "I think he *loves* the work for Z5, and if we can share it, so much the better."

"If you're of the same mind a month from now, you'll be the most welcome new agent we've had in years." Palfrey told her.

Their flight to London was called and they said goodbye to Stefan, who saw the others to the aircraft first, then stood aside with Palfrey while the main stream of passengers got on board. The engines of other aircraft were roaring, jet engines giving their high-pitched growls on landing or the shrieking as they took off. Into a lull, Stefan said:

"Such a noise, Sap! How we could use silence!"

"Yes," Palfrey said. "Yes."

"Is that really why you hesitated about the best thing to do?"

"Yes," Palfrey replied. "That and the decontamination of the radio-active air. They had so much power for positive good, I wondered — and I shall always wonder whether we could have used it for good and not evil. The boon of silence could be as great as any we've known."

"Sap," Stefan said.

"You think I'm wrong," remarked Palfrey.

"Not truly," answered Stefan. "I think there were two ways of looking at this and we happened to be on different sides." He nodded to an official who came up, obviously to ask Palfrey to board, and put out his left hand. "Sap — when you can, and when we are not under pressure, come and spend a while here so that we can talk."

"I'll do that," Palfrey promised. "I'll do that just as soon as I can."

He shook hands . . .

He saw Stefan standing near the steps which were moved from the loading bay as the aircraft taxied off, and the huge man was still there when Palfrey looked back for the last time. He saw Janey, hand-in-hand with Philip, and he wondered whether they would be wise to work together for Z5. He did not disturb them, and soon dozed off. When he woke as they were about to land at London airport, the others were asleep, Janey's head on Philip's shoulder. But both were alert enough when they disembarked at London and they walked together along the interminable glass-walled corridors to the customs hall and then out into the main airport.

"You two go on to Chelsea," Palfrey said, "and spend a few days at the house at Romain Square. I'll see you at headquarters before long."

"That's a very good idea," Philip said warmly.

Janey kissed Palfrey very firmly on the lips and then got into one of two Z5 cars which were waiting. He got into one, helped by the Jamaican driver, who drove in welcome silence to the West End. Joyce Morgan would be up and waiting. All the routine work would be ticking over. From all over the world reports would be coming in. It was even conceivable that one of them would herald a threat as great as the one just passed.

Threat?

Joyce *was* waiting; concerned, solicitous.

Z5 was working normally.

"Sap," Joyce said, "there's just one thing before you go to bed, one thing you must know." He could tell from her manner that this was good, not bad news. "There is to be a summit meeting of all the great powers, to discuss what happened here and in Russia, and to try again to work together. So this has done some good, even if it's only another attempt."

Another chance, thought Palfrey. Yes, it was good. It might even be the beginning of true peace between nations, but — it might also be the last chance.

That was what he feared so much: that when the last chance came the leaders of the world would lack the wisdom to take and use it as best it could be used.

STAR-BEGOTTEN by H.G. Wells

A rare classic from The Master. An unseen intelligence from the stars was manipulating human genes to produce a race of supermen on earth.

95394—95¢

THE HIGH CRUSADE
by
Poul Anderson

Science fiction with a twist. An epic tale of a mighty race of warriors that takes place 600 years in the *past*. A fabulous journey to the infinite reaches of the imagination!

95374—95¢

Manor Books Inc.
432 Park Avenue South
New York, New York 10016

Please send me the MB books I have checked above. I am enclosing $_____ Check or money order, (no currency or C.O.D.'s). Enclose price listed for each title plus 25¢ per copy ordered to cover cost of postage and handling.

☐ Send me a free list of all your books in print.

Name _____

Address _____

City_____ State_____ Zip _____

DEATH IS MY SHADOW
by Edward S. Aarons

All Pete wanted was a woman. He found plenty—every one beautiful to behold and dangerous to the touch. Soon, Pete's innocent fancies became a trapdoor to brutality and ever-widening circles of death.

95371—95¢